THE
BLACK ACES
MC

S COURTNEY

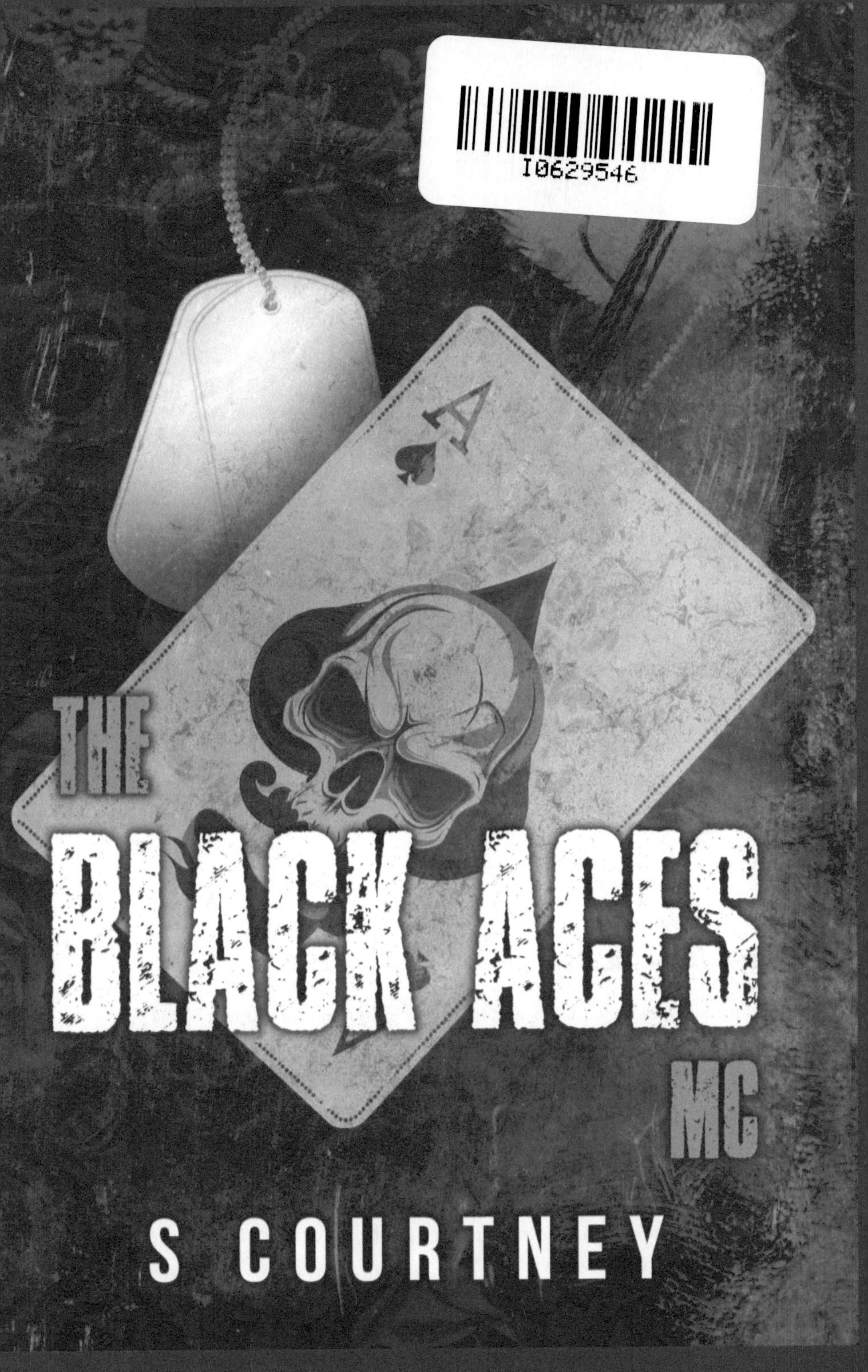

The Black Aces

Jackal (Leader)
Digi
Knox
Blondie
Cupid
Club
Cheetah

Location: Van Hollen, New Mexico

Warning: Sexual harassment, blood, graphic violence, death, explicit language, gun violence, loss of limb, kidnapping

Trigger: threat of rape, physical violence

Cupid

Listen, I don't care for money or finding out who I really am or any of that. All I need is my cut, my bike, and my boys.

To hell with everything else... especially love.

I didn't survive 29 years of my miserable, down and out, sorry ass life to be brought down by some reckless emotion that stole my mother from me. No way in hell, life is fucked up and, in the end, you die, point A to point B, no room for detours.

Well, enough about that.

I guess I should introduce myself. I am Aleister McElroy, a loyal member of the Black Aces Motorcycle Club out of Van Hollen, New Mexico.

We're a unique club. No assigned roles; everyone pitches in, enforces rules, handles business, and deals with anyone who steps out of line. No need for titles.

In our team, there are individuals who have expertise in specific areas, for instance, Digi, a computer genius. Barely legal when he took down Google in the snap of a finger one Christmas a few years back just to see if he could. He loved a good challenge. The kid cracked their security and firewall in less than five minutes, so they knew they weren't immune no matter how much they thought they owned the internet. The media frenzy was insane, that crazy bastard! He's just as good as those global hackers, and I'm thankful he's on our side.

Then there's Cheetah, the fastest gunslinger I've ever seen. He would have reigned supreme in the Wild West of the mid-1600's. His accuracy is deadly too; it's like he has crosshairs embedded in his hazel eyes. I don't think I've seen him miss, ever.

And then there's me, always ready to throw hands. I expected my six-foot-four stature, dark eyes, long hair and beard, and many tattoos and piercings to get me a strong club name like Tarzan or Thor, cause I favored both, but what name did they choose for me?

Cupid, fucking Cupid.

I swear I thought they were kidding, but judging by Jackal's stern expression, they weren't. Those bastards I call my brothers gave me that nickname as a joke, because 'fuck love' has always been my mantra.

Every single stomach-churning aspect, a nauseating swirl of bitter bile and regret, except the brotherly kind, they were like a warm, comforting blanket in my darkest hours.

Seriously, look at me, do I look like some fat cherub fuck who shoots his load covered arrows at people so they can act stupid about another human? No way, but that's the label they chose for me, and rookies are expected to accept it without protest. Jackasses, I'm far from love, loving anyone, or anything.

That's how you keep safe, lock away all that emotional stuff and never show it. That's what I do.

Or so I thought.

Saturday 6:00 pm Black Aces Clubhouse

We're chilling at the clubhouse, drinking the night away with a few club bunnies scattered around and flirting with their marks for the night.

If you don't know, club bunnies are women who like to "service" the bike club members hoping to switch over to ol' lady status, but the number one rule is never wife a club skank. Ever.

They were only there for a good time.

Back to the current surroundings, Cheetah had a feisty one grinding on his lap, her barely there skirt riding up to the lace of her black boy shorts. She shoves her tongue down his throat as he grabs her ass hard, causing her to squeal. She was a petite little thing. I think her name was Mandy, with curvaceous hips, fiery red hair, and the most emerald eyes I have ever seen. Judging by how hot and heavy it was getting, they'd be leaving soon. His cocky smirk, a self-satisfied curve of his lips, said it all.

Blondie had two bunnies competing for his dick tonight. I always thought he and I got our nicknames to tease us, but he used it to his advantage. He had platinum blond hair that offset his tan skin and blue eyes. If it weren't for the UV damage from the rides, he could easily be a model for the world's top designers. He was our resident pretty boy, and Trixie was arguing with Lolli about who got to fuck him.

Trix was an overly proportionate dirty blonde with an unhealthy obsession with the tanning bed or baking in the sun. I swear she would eerily glow in the dark.

Yeah, I fucked her, but she was an extremely loud bore

of a woman. How someone can ride you and be deadweight beats me. She exerted no effort but wailed like a banshee, like I was pounding her pussy out and trust me, I was using nowhere near my full potential. Why waste good dick energy?

I have never considered ever doing this until that one time with her. I had to do it. I had to fake it to get her to shut up. Threw in a few pants and 'Jesus woman, you sure know how to wear a man out'. I immediately went to the bathroom to discard the "used" condom and flush it so she wouldn't see the evidence, or lack thereof.

Yeah, men fake it, too. I'll never admit it goes to the grave with me.

Lolli, on the other hand, holy fuck! They didn't call her that for nothing. If you needed your soul sucked from your body as she brought you to your knees, then she's your girl. When I needed a quick blow, I always picked Lolli. She was a petite brunette with hazel eyes and a Hoover vacuum for a mouth.

She would start slowly with light teasing licks, swirling around, and then she would take you into her mouth and suck the tip like a pacifier until she had you growling in frustrated pleasure. After that, she went for the kill and took you to the hilt.

No. Gag. Reflex.

I can't explain, but her throat was like a warm, soft, vice grip and she wasn't backing down until you emptied down her throat. She always had a smug look afterwards, like she knew she owned a piece of your soul as she licked her lips clean of any evidence that didn't make it into her mouth.

Fuck, I got to stop thinking about our last hookup. I can't tend bar with a stiff dick.

I was behind the counter, drying the freshly washed glasses, as the girls sat on each of Blondie's knees. As usual, he didn't wear a shirt under his cut, or our club vest. He knew what he was doing by gratuitously displaying his broad chest and muscular arms, stoking the fire. He sits back while watching the claws come out.

"Don't be a greedy whore. You fucked him yesterday, Trixie! Tonight it's my turn, and you know we're not allowed here during church tomorrow so piss off and find another dick to fuck!" Lolli stared Trix down with fire in her eyes, she wasn't wavering and if Trix knew better, she'd go elsewhere and make some bastard her second choice.

Trix holds her hands up and hops off his knee, conceding defeat. Her eyes started wandering around and met mine for a quick second. I shook my head. *Keep it moving,* as her eyes scan who's left and her smile widens as she looks at Jackal, our leader.

If I ever aged as gracefully as Jackal did, I'd be one lucky son of a bitch. His jet-black hair slicked back but his beard was almost fully grey, tattoos telling the many stories of his hardened life, and a sense of hardcore rebel badass radiated from him. He was six foot three of muscle and charm, but one thing he didn't do was club bunnies. He let us horny bastards have them around, but he never partook.

He was a grief-stricken man with a broken heart. He lost his ol' lady four years ago to cancer. Even though I despised love, I adored Miss Paige, the sweetest lady to be around; she was like a mother to me, but then cancer took her, and I hated the world for taking yet another soul from me.

I've lost everyone I've ever cared about.

I remember walking into the clubhouse and smelling

Paige's famous teriyaki meatballs and homemade mashed potatoes dripping in butter, sour cream, and chives.

"Oh man, Paige, you always cook the best meals! You're the sweetest person I know." I'd say, kissing her cheek. She'd smile over her shoulder as she watched me stuff my face.

"Well, I got to keep my boys fed. You know, you're all my children, even my old man there. Biggest child of them all, but I love the big lug."

She'd chuckle while starting on her homemade, from scratch dessert. She would bake mouth watering lemon bars, giant gooey cinnamon rolls, or her world-famous cinnamon apple bake.

What I wouldn't give to have her around, even for one day. I know Jackal would, too.

He reacted like any distraught, heartbroken shell of a man would, and it took days for us to convince him to eat, weeks for us to get him out the bed and showered. He had given up like he wanted to die and honestly, with a love like that, I couldn't blame him, but that's not what Miss Paige would have wanted.

The battle to keep him alive was relentless. We carried him to the bathtub, scrubbed his feverish skin, his body creating a sickness physically to mirror his emotional grief. The rhythm of the washcloth was a counterpoint to his ragged sobs over his lost love.

Today, he's better but definitely not ready for affection of any sort and that was crystal clear to everyone, including the bunnies, but Trix was hardheaded. She would not back down, hoping to bag the Prez, wearing it as a badge of honor.

She and her five-inch stilettos stumble over and she awkwardly flails into his lap. He stares at her while she giggles and flirts, leaning forward to whisper something in his ear, running her finger down his arm. He looks at his arm when she leans back. She's grinning from ear to ear until he pulls her closer, whispering something back. All the color drains from her face. She jumps off his lap and runs out of the house, but no one really reacts until the door slams shut. Her friends didn't go after her and the guys kept drinking.

Jackal continued casually sipping the remaining scotch and signaled to me for another. I nodded as I prepared the chilled glass and square block of ice, pouring the smooth amber liquid, causing the cube to crack a bit. Whatever he said to make her scram wasn't pretty, that I'm sure of.

I step from behind the bar and hand him his drink. "Damn, Prez, what did you say to her? She booked it out of here like those girls being chased in a horror movie."

He took a long sip, taking a moment to savor it. "I merely put her in her place." He didn't say another word.

I saw movement out of the corner of my eye, and I watched Blondie head upstairs with Lolli. He was in for a wild ride. Lolli squealed as he lifted her up on his hip and palmed her ass as she slammed her lips on him, moaning loudly. Blondie snapped his fingers my way, signaling he needed another beer, judging by the intensity I gave him a pair of them. She winks at me as she takes one bottle while Blondie makes his way up the stairs.

Lucky bastard.

Not that I wanted to take her from him, but I could use a release. It had been three weeks and Lolli had done a fucking number on me.

Of course, my dick conspired with my mind to remind me of that night. It was the early morning hours, like 3 am, when we stumbled up the stairs. I slammed her against my door, shutting it at the same time. She pushed me into the corner by the door and went to work after she got my jeans down.

I didn't care to lock my dick behind more fabric, so it sprung free, almost hitting her in the face.

She chuckled as she licked her lips in response. "I see Cupid's arrow could use some attention. It's so big and thick. Mmm..."

She took me by surprise by taking it back all the way instead of her usual teasing. My legs wobbled, the cool, rough wall a welcome brace against my trembling body. My breath hitched, shallow and rapid, as my fingers tangled in her hair, urging her closer, deeper, though she was already bottomed out. The sensation was electric, a white-hot wave, an overwhelming need I couldn't, wouldn't, resist.

"Fuck, baby, yeah, just like that. Put those filthy lips to work."

She grins as much as she can with a mouth full, then she tightens her grip and all I remember is blacking out and grunting. When I came to, she had her shorts pulled down, no panties, and I gripped her hips tightly, lifted her, and slammed her back into me hard. She yelped as I tore her shirt off and undid her bra to spring those gorgeous breasts free, squeezing and twisting her nipples. The multitude of sensations flooding her senses left her reeling, but I held her steady as I rammed deep inside her.

She was my means to an end, and that's it. She toppled over, wrapping her arms around my shoulders, screaming my name to the heavens before she came all over me. She leans forward against me, panting, trying to kiss me.

With the girls, one thing I never engage in is intimacy.

I turned away, and she caught my cheek.

"Aww, what's the matter you don't *love* when I kiss you?"
She finally got the strength to stand on her own.

"I don't love, and you know that. Suck and fuck, that's it."

I slid past her so I could take a piss. She scoffs while putting herself back together. She steals a shirt of mine since I destroyed hers and twists it up and folds the excess under to make a sexy crop top.

"Say what you want, but you have a name inspired by a well-known ode to love and it's not ironic...but what do I know?"

She watches me as I continue to piss with the door open. I refuse to acknowledge the statement, so she flips me the bird before giggling as she leaves.

Damn club bunnies think they know me. Only my brothers know the actual story...the real Aleister.

Just our conversation stirs up the memories of my mom and her issues that I've been trying to bury for so long...

Eleven years earlier

I have to keep reminding myself that she is my mother, and I am an adult.

Deep breaths, man. Just see what she wants.

"Aleister Conrad McElroy, bring yourself here this instant!"

My mother's familiar shrill voice echoed through the house. I found her in the living room with a stranger. I stopped dead in my tracks, staring.

Tall, dark, and handsome, he exuded intensity from his dark, sandy brown hair to his piercing gaze. His expensive suit, and the silk pocket square that likely cost more than his sofa, spoke volumes.

Looks like mom nabbed herself a rich one this time.

A look of shock crossed the man's face as he looked from my beaming mother to me.

"Aleister, come here, honey." She held her hand out like I was five years old and we were about to cross a busy intersection.

I brushed past her hand and shocked expression, taking a seat in the chair facing the couch. I didn't like the feeling; something didn't sit well with me about this stranger. His gaze was competitive, and if he was after my mother's affection, he'd soon learn I never back down.

"Aleister, this is my... friend, Mr. Wellington. Carey, my son, Aleister." Her voice caught on the "my," I noticed.

I watched her stiffen and plaster on her fake smile when she was trying to hide something.

He, Mr. Wellington, merely nodded.

I wasn't up for playing games..

"Okay, what the hell is this?"

"Aleister! Language! Don't speak like that in front of...company like that."

"It's okay, Diane," he said, patting her knee but keeping his stern expression fixed on me. "It's teenage rebellion." I roll my eyes and then focus back on her.

"Spit it out, mother, why am I here?" I try to give her some semblance of respect. I loved my mother, as any child should, but her taste in men was questionable. He was just another one, but in a flashy suit; no one was ever good enough for her.

She crosses her legs at the ankles and angles her body

towards him as she takes his hand. "Mr. Wellington and I are...old friends and we've decided to see one another."

"Okay." I said bluntly.

"Well, I want you to get to know him better and you two can bond over things you have in common."

I scoffed. "I doubt we have *anything* in common except you, and I'm sure you'll be banging him in no time. So, are we done here?" I looked away before I could see the shock on both their faces. I didn't care to be a part of whatever this charade was.

They began whispering to each other, and I only caught pieces, "...your temper...you left...not yet", was all I could decipher but, to be honest, at the tender age of 18, I didn't give a shit.

Who she did was none of my concern.

I was almost done with this chapter of my life. I couldn't wait to leave this bumblefuck town. I looked back over, and he was kissing her hand and she was giggling... *here we go.*

My mom was always getting into no good relationships with men. Let's start with the dirty lowlife scumbag who knocked her up and then left her to fend for herself and a child. If I ever met him, I'd kill him myself! She worked tirelessly as she provided everything she could and sacrificed so much of herself so that I had a normal life.

Through that, I was always there to pick up her shattered pieces. I was her only constant. With each decline in her physical and emotional strength, she distanced herself further, leaving me feeling increasingly isolated. Was this going to be the time she shuts me out forever? I hoped not, but it was out of my hands.

I look over and they are all kissy-kissy, making me nauseous.

"Can I go now?" I wanted to be as far from her bedroom as possible. I knew where this was going. I planned to sleep in my old treehouse in the backyard. The horror of knowing how loud my mom is, I knew to bring my radio and headphones. I shudder at the thought.

She nods and I extend an olive branch. I turn to head to my room to gather my stuff. "Nice to meet you, Mr. Wellington."

Later...

Well, I knew it. And now the whole damn neighborhood knows.

My mother is a screamer.

Why am I being tortured?! This is emotional trauma!

Anyway, I could hear his hardcore grunts and her wailing through music blasting in my headphones and a pillow over my head.

Holy fucking hell, I'm not even in the house where it probably echoes off the walls. I thought I had picked the lesser of two evils until I looked out to see him plowing himself into my mother through her open window. That's why I can hear him clear as day.

He's sweating profusely, making her call him daddy, and screaming his name as he smacked her ass. I lay back down and crank the music to blast out as much as I could so I could survive another day.

By the time I came in the next morning, he's already gone, but the smile on her face was not.

Here we go.

"Good morning, honey." She kisses me on the cheek as

she piles the pancakes and bacon on my plate. She's already falling for him. All the blaring warning signs were there.

I stab my fork into the stack of warm, buttery goodness as she floats around the kitchen. She was cheery and humming while she cleaned up.

This better be for her good. I don't know how much more she could take.

Sadly, I would get my answer soon...

Present Day

Bang bang

"Let's call church to order. It'll be a short one today."

Jackal hated long drawn out meetings, get to the point and get out. Also, he liked to visit Paige on some Sundays and important milestones like her birthday and their anniversary. The only time we left him completely alone.

He puffs his Montecristo corona cigar before continuing. "So, we still need to enforce this pact with Johnny and his douche bag lackeys, and we're not going to fight again. I will not be dragged into a bloodbath over a pissing contest, so Cupid, you'll take Cheetah and Blondie to sign the treaty. You're meeting with them the day after tomorrow."

I bolt up, "Wait, why me? You know the bad blood between that fucker and me. I'd rather break his goddamn neck."

Johnny Picardio was a psychopath, a druggie given far too much power. He started his own gang on the other side of town and was immediately hostile towards us because of me.

Johnny didn't give a shit about her, but my mom, of course, devoted everything to him and he didn't even deserve to be spit on if he was on fire.

I never sugar coat my hatred for that bastard. I wanted to castrate him lengthwise when I found out he slept around while dating my mom. I should have known his slimy ass wouldn't be able to stay faithful. I know he was the final nail in her coffin.

Let's talk about the big blow-up; one day, a much younger blonde knocked on my mother's door and blindsided her, claiming a months-long affair with Johnny. My mother called her a liar until the girl described Johnny's intimate details. Apparently, he has a tattoo of a dagger near his dick.

After the confrontation, she waited for him and waited for him at the door. She screamed at him while he tried to deflect, claiming they were never exclusive, that he never agreed to *only* see her. He said it with an icy stare in his steely blue eyes and you could physically see her heart shatter once again.

I pummeled that slimy fucker's face the next time I saw him until my boys pulled me off. I don't regret a single blow.

He swore he'd kill me, but Jackal stopped everything and negotiated a temporary order of peace. Guess now was time to make it official and put it to paper, four years after that incident.

I'll never shake his hand. He's the reason she's dead.

I look back to see Jackal, his jaw tight. "You WILL go because I said so. Don't forget who runs this club, me not you, so you will do as I say, got it?!" His voice boomed against the walls.

I sat down, defeated, but didn't cower. "Yeah, boss."

"Good." He hands me the peace treaty with his signature on it. Guess I have no choice, fuck I hate that druggie bastard.

Lyric

"Hey Lyric! Move your sweet ass with our drinks! I swear women are only good for one thing and they can't even do that right, ain't that right, sweetheart?"

I slam his drinks down on their wobbly table and glare, stupid strung out asshole, wish I didn't need this job, but I have to pay my bills. It's a sad life I live.

"Hey sweetness, when are you going to let me see if you got a strong gag reflex for all this?" He points to his dick as they all laugh at his empty chauvinism.

I probably wouldn't even feel it. Like twiddling a toothpick.

I pick up the tray instead of what I really wanted to do, which was headbutt him in the fucking face, and go back to the bar. He was an idiot, but still dangerous, especially when high on whatever he could find; I couldn't risk it.

I hate him, his club, and most of all, my life, but until I could save enough to get away, I was stuck listening to this inept peon brag about things that never happened. Especially the lie that I blew him in the bar bathroom. I'd rather slice off my right breast with a rusty tuna can lid than have that loser touch me.

I checked my watch quickly, it's 4pm and of course, the alcoholics were gathering early to get their liquid add fix.

Cinnamon Alley was the only bar in town. Too bad, because I'd love to not see some of these scumbags.

What I wouldn't give to be living on a beach somewhere, or anywhere that isn't the middle of nowhere New Mexico.

If I hadn't been abandoned here by my so-called loving boyfriend, I would have had a better life, but I made mistake after mistake, especially in trusting that jackass with my future. The bitter taste of betrayal coated my tongue, a physical manifestation of the continuing resentment churning in my gut. My shoulders slumped at the weight of my naivety pressing down on my chest, making it hard to breathe.

He promised me a better life, a promise he never intended to keep.

We left the slums of Millington, Texas, and headed West towards my dream of living in sunny California. I was too excited to see the warning signs. I was enjoying the wind in my hair as we put as much space between us and our old town. Nothing there but crackheads and their dealers and unfortunately, I was riding with one, but he swore he was getting clean and I believed him. Kind of, because prior to me being abandoned, I was smart enough to stash $500 in my shoe when we stopped for gas and he went inside to pay.

He had stolen and pawned enough stuff for me to second guess his journey to getting clean, but I still had hope. He was taking me away from it all.

So, I continued playing naïve to make a new life. I didn't think it would be in this go-nowhere town of Van Hollen. Fuck my life.

He took my cash, my car, and everything of value early one morning while I was asleep, leaving me in that dirty, seedy motel room with only my cell phone, my clothes, and the money I hid under the insole of my sneaker.

Not like he answered my frantic hysterical calls, anyway. Wherever he went, he better stay there. I've got plenty of ideas of how to make him suffer and squeal like a pig.

It won't be pretty.

I am forever in debt to Dave for taking in a broken, crying mess of a girl to tend his bar and save money. After hearing my tearful story, he unexpectedly hired me, and in doing so, saved my life. I even got myself a tiny apartment nearby. I've gotten a bit of my life back, but I still can't wait to leave.

Dumb fuck is snapping his privileged fingers for another round, sanctimonious asshole. I turn to pour the beers when the saloon doors open with force, slamming loudly against the frame. I jump at the sudden sound, almost knocking over the mugs. I look up to see a pack of big brawny guys walk in with leather vests on.

Definitely the motorcycle club I had heard about, not like Johnny's band of misfits. They were an intimidating presence. The man in front scanned the room, clearly searching for someone. I wouldn't want to be that person.

Now, I'm not looking for anything in the least bit as far as a relationship, but he was a handsome, tall drink of water. His long, dark blonde hair fell past his shoulders. A thick, sexy beard, rough to the touch, framed a firm jaw. Muscular arms, a tapestry of inked designs, hinted at power and a wild history. Boy, I'd like to read that book.

As he scans the area, his dark eyes meet mine for a split second, but he sneers at me like I wronged him.

What the hell? Do I have to deal with another set of assholes? Focus, Lyric, you need to earn money.

Tarzan, because that's who he resembles, looks like he found his target.

Holy shit, it's Johnny!

They're looking for Johnny! Please, put a bullet in his head, for all our sakes. Watching, I only see one visible weapon; a holstered gun on the one to the far right. At least one of them is carrying a weapon.

Beating him to a bloody pulp is also a delicious option. The first round of drinks would be on me!

Tarzan walks towards Johnny and his rowdy bunch, who stop all conversation. The tension is thick as dark, billowing smoke from the depths of hell. My intuition tells me to stay back and observe.

Johnny leans back, putting his arm behind the chair. "Well, look who we have here, Cupid and his precious cherubs. What the hell do ya want?"

Tarzan didn't take kindly to the barb. He closed his eyes and took a deep breath before he sneered at him, then grabbed a chair, turned it, and sat with his arms leaning forward against the back. His stare was cold, calculating, like he was trying to maintain his composure.

Ooh, there's definitely some history there. He produces a piece of paper from his upper vest pocket and slams it down.

"You know why I'm here. Sign the treaty so we can get out of this shit hole."

Wow, rude, but damn if his voice and underlying tone are sexy as fuck. Imagine how he is in... *calm down, it's been a while, those are your hormones talking.*

Johnny looks at the guy to the left of him. "What? You don't want a drink? A peace offering between clubs."

Johnny snaps his fingers to signal he wanted me to bring that round. How was I going to balance eight bottles without looking like an idiot? Shit!

"No Johnny, I'd rather ram my fist down your fucking throat, but my Prez makes the rules, so sign the damn document."

The air crackled with tension, making it impossible to misinterpret Tarzan's intense, burning hatred for Johnny. I was curious to know why. But first, to get these drinks there without embarrassing myself in front of the sexy biker beast.

Every one of them was a looker in their own way, the platinum blonde could model all over the world with his distinct good looks, he didn't have my pulse racing, no it was jungle boy, who never took his eyes off the group in front of him. His jaw clenched every second he had to be in Johnny's presence.

I chose to carry four bottles at once, hearing the gentle clinking as I walked. I placed the first set in front of Johnny. He takes that moment to be bold and smack my ass.

"Thank you, sweetness. Now get the rest. Chop chop!" He smirks, but I was furious. Tarzan didn't seem fazed by it either, or he was great at poker, because he showed no emotion.

I growled as I walked back to retrieve the rest.

Johnny leans back and rests his arm across the back of his chair. "This doesn't change shit between us, Cupid. I'll get my hands on you one way or another and shut you up for good." He sneered, but it didn't faze his opponent.

"Your goddamned right it doesn't, you insensitive cock-sucker! You broke her heart. You are the reason she's dead!"

"It's not my fault she was a delusional crackpot..."

I gasped and dropped the drinks because a melee was

happening in front of me! Before me, a chaotic blur of flailing limbs and grunts erupted. Tarzan's brutal force slammed Johnny's head against the hard wood of the table; a sickening thud echoed in the sudden silence. Blows landed with sharp cracks and heavy thuds, a dizzying whirlwind of motion too fast to follow. My eyes, however, locked onto Tarzan, a desperate attempt to grasp the brutal ballet unfolding before me.

He took good care of Johnny, mostly targeting his body and sparing a few hits to his face. I guess he didn't want his Prez, as he referred to him, to witness Johnny's face looking like a car wreck.

After one of Johnny's associates tried a cheap shot, Blonde boy, with fists like ice blocks, knocked him out cold. Blondie then went to work trying to peel Tarzan's fists off of Johnny. He kept screaming that he killed her, that she'd be alive if it weren't for him.

I wonder who she was to him? Either way, it was bad if he was here to negotiate, and now we were in the middle of a brawl.

BANG

Everyone froze as Dave fired his shotgun, the smoke billowing from the barrel and debris falling from the ceiling. The shell clang echoing as it bounced off the bar top.

I couldn't stop the scream that slipped from my lips. I never heard anything so loud! My ears are ringing...

Tarzan pulls back while Johnny tries to figure out where he is. In a daze, I grab the beers, fully aware that Johnny will probably ask for them in his pissed-off state, likely trying to drink away his pain. I place them on the counter, trying to get myself to move.

"Fun's over gentlemen, you will not tear up my bar any

further. Aces, I suggest you leave and Johnny, you leave out the other way. Go on now!" Johnny sits back in his chair, watching the Aces back away, never breaking eye contact.

I was scared he'd get mad if I didn't bring the rest of the beer, so I did.I could barely steady my shaking hands as I gently put down the two bottles. He snatches one, startling me. As Tarzan finally turns around to leave, Johnny's lips pull together in a smirk while he pulls a gun from inside his coat and aims it.He chuckled, his smile covered in blood.

Holy shit! He's going to kill him!

I acted without thinking, grabbed the other beer bottle, and smashed it over his head. The glass shatters and Johnny's out with one blow. He slumps over onto the table. His associates were looking up at the opposite side of the room with absolute fear in their eyes, their hands up, unwilling to move.

My gaze followed, and I looked right into the barrel of the gunslinger, who was about a millisecond from blowing Johnny's brains out.

Shit, he was fast!

I dropped my tray in fear, hoping he wouldn't accidentally shoot me instead.

Uh oh.

Everybody's staring at me as Johnny's buddy checks him over. He groans. The fucker's still alive. Gunslinger puts his pistol away but looks at me and tips his head as if he had a hat on. I nod back.

My eyes then meet Tarzan's and I expected appreciation or a thank you, a nod of appreciation, but do you know what I got? He walks up to me, essentially towering over me. His hair fanning over his face as he growls, still breathing hard. I found my breath almost matching.

"Cheetah had me covered; I didn't need your help."

Well...excuse the fuck outta me!

I erupted in anger, saying whatever came to mind. I was tired of all this testosterone fueled, macho bullshit!

"You're welcome, you self-righteous asshole! Looks like I beat him to the punch. Who's the fucking cheetah now?"

Whhhhhy couldn't I keep my trap shut?

Pissing off a handsomely rugged, violent man was not my intention. His eyes darkened more as he looked down at me condescendingly.

"Listen, *Princess*, I didn't need your goddamned help! You put your little nose where it doesn't belong. I suggest you stay out of my business and watch that filthy mouth of yours."

I stood taller, "Make me!"

That took the wind out of his sails. He murmurs something, turns, and walks out, leaving me to deal with the consequences of my actions... and my boss.

Shit.

Cupid

I have to confess; the speed of her reaction was impressive. I don't know if I would have walked out that bar if it wasn't for her, but I can't think about that now. I was up Schitt's Creek with Jackal. I really screwed up.

He shouldn't have sent me in the first place! I also shouldn't have let my emotions take over. Well, time to face the music cause the evidence is all over my bruised and bloody hands. I think one of those bastards split my lip.

Jackal was sitting at the kitchen table drinking a cup of coffee. He stopped sipping when he saw us all. I sprinkle the torn pieces of the treaty on the table in front of him and exhale, "I'm sorry, boss."

He eyes the pieces, my hands, and sighs loudly. It was full of disappointment.

"I asked you to do this because I know how much you loathe him, but I know how much you care for the club that took you in after she died. I needed you to bury the hatchet, and you might have started the war." He stands up and claps his hand on my shoulder.

"It will never be over until that bastard is dead by my hands. Did you know he almost shot me today! That spineless coward pulled a gun when I turned my back to leave. There would have been a war either way."

The guys all back up my claim. Jackal looks around, nodding at Cheetah. "Did Wyatt Earp there finish the job? Is he dead?"

Naturally, that's the assumption when Cheetah's on the job.

Cheetah lets out a low chuckle that sounds like a grumble. "Oh, believe me, I had him in my sights, but someone beat me to the punchline. Cute little thing, too. I think she has eyes for Cupid and his...arrow. Couldn't take her eyes off him once we stepped into the bar. I watched it the whole time." A grin formed before it quickly disappeared.

Someone stifled their laughs, but I remained heated. How that little tart was so quick to react beats me. I bring myself out of my thoughts just as Blondie spoke up while grabbing a couple of cold ones from behind the bar.

"Yeah Jackal, you should have seen this girl.

She might have been tiny, but she swung the bottle like a pro baseball player at the World Series. Frankly, Johnny should be dead or severely brain-damaged. He's likely been tormenting her, and she seized the chance for revenge." Blondie passes me a beer before plopping down on the sofa with a sly smile in my direction.

He continues, "If I didn't know any better, she wants to..."

"You can shut your trap. Don't even finish that sentence."

Yeah, cut them off before they can taunt me any further. I wasn't in the mood. This beer wasn't strong enough, and my hands hurt like a motherfucker.

I stand and grab a bottle of Jack before heading upstairs without another word. Just the wandering thought of a certain bartender with fire in her eyes.

She was affecting more than my mind and I needed to get a handle on all of it, especially my dick.

Lyric

"Lyric, honey, why don't you head home and get some rest." I turn to see Dave watching me try to frantically clean up the mess and make up for my actions. I needed this job.

He takes my shaky hands. "I'm not going to fire you. You saved Cupid's life; Johnny deserved what he got. There's always been bad blood between them, but don't worry about that. I'll see you in the morning."

Tears pool in my eyes, but I refuse to cry. I look at him and nod before he pulls me in for a hug. I sigh and relax into a feeling I hadn't felt in a while, comfort.

I put the bar towel down, grab my things, and head for the door, but stop.

"Wait, is Cupid his actual name?" I turn to ask Dave.

"Yeah, his club name. He's a cold-hearted son of a bitch who detests the word love and everything about it. The irony, huh?" He chuckles as he sets the chairs knocked over back right.

He left me with a lot to think about but, hardened bastard or not, he owes me a thank you and I'm going to get it, dammit!

Cupid

Jack Daniels isn't strong enough for the physical pain I'm experiencing. I can't take aspirin and incur the wrath of mixing pills and booze, so now I lay here and my left hand has a throbbing fucking pulse, a strong one at that. I open and close it several times, hoping to get some relief.

Today was truly a shit show. Now we're definitely on alert for retaliation. Since Johnny showed no remorse, it's now kill or be killed, and I wasn't going down without a fight.

I lay on top of my covers shirtless, teasing my nipple piercings. I do that when I'm severely in need. I can feel my dick throbbing with the dire need to be stroked, but I was in no mood for a quickie or dealing with any of the bunnies. I would take care of myself.

I sighed as I shut my eyes to the world and allowed my hand to slip down into my boxers as I hissed, letting the carnal fantasy unfold in my head.

I don't mean to brag, but my "arrow," as the bunnies called it, required some maneuvering to free it, yet it felt great to have some friction and movement around it.

I stiffened between my grasp, sighing as I heard her breathless voice. Her gasps and moans of my name were heavenly to my ears, but yet to see my vision.

An image slowly appeared, and I'll be damned if it wasn't the bargirl. I know it's what I wanted but didn't expect to see her draped in an oversized, flowy white silk robe. And then she undid the tie and let it pool at her feet. I followed the delicate fabric to the floor before my eyes feasted on the prize. She was petite, maybe five foot three or four, with reddish dirty blonde hair that stopped above her nipples. She stared at me with her sapphire blue eye, playing with her full perky breasts and perfect nipples you wanted to feast on. Suddenly, she was on my lap riding me while I listened to her cries of undoing. Her curves were as deadly as a winding highway road. She gasped to her own touch, never taking her gaze off me.

I quickened my pace, feeling my body heat up, my muscles tense, and my ragged breathing a prelude to climax.

She continued to stare at me as her hand wandered down between her soft heaving chest, her thumb brushing against her nipple, down her taut stomach, until she gasped as she teased her pussy and whispered my name. She moaned my name so deliciously; I couldn't hold back. It was an explosion, the likes I never had before. Even after my main release, I had aftershock releases, each one racking my body.

I'd be grunting her name if I knew it. But what triggered this fantasy was the glare she gave Johnny when he smacked her ass. Her frigid stare caused a stir within me. I should have shriveled up in fear, but it made me hard as a rock.

After my climax, I showered and slipped on another pair

of boxers and went to bed hoping to be in much less pain in the morning.

Lyric

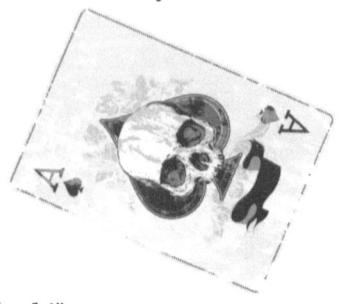

"Oh... yes, yes! Fuck!"

I can't stop. I swear I hear his deep gravelly voice command me in my ear, "Come for me, kitten. All over those pretty little fingers and I'll lap them up." My nipples are deliciously sore from teasing and pinching as I thought about him savagely taking me repeatedly until I couldn't come anymore.

He'd gather my hair in his hand and pull deliciously rough. I loved a little pain with my pleasure, while I ran my nails down his tattoo laden back, marking my territory like he liked to mark his skin. He'd growl to the sensation because fuck, he loved that.

His hair or his scratchy beard would brush against my nipples, causing a gasp. I fantasized about him having pierced nipples, adorned with silver barbells, to complete his hardcore biker image. I'd tug on his piercings while he was pounding into me until he came so hard he collapsed on top of me. Only our labored breathing breaks the silence.

I couldn't take it anymore.

I moaned as my fingers slid in and out of my soaking wet pussy at lightning speed. The feeling was euphoric, and I only craved more until my legs shook and I saw stars.

I knew nothing about him other than he was good looking and had a crap nickname. And that he yelled at me like I was a damn child and I wasn't having it. He *was gonna* apologize and thank me for saving his life or there'd be hell to pay.

Coming down from my orgasm, I was breathing erratically. My skin was on fire, a light sheen to it, and warm to the touch. I guess I should thank him for my strongest orgasm to date. I needed it and now I needed sleep.

Tomorrow was another day, and I was going to find the Black Aces headquarters and get what's owed to me.

Cupid

I woke up and my hands felt better. I rub them across my face, but pause when I hear a ruckus downstairs.

Like shouting.

Morning bunny drama: it's a territorial dispute over dick, I know it. Whose is it this time? My curiosity gets the best of me. I get up and stretch, foregoing clothes. I didn't want to miss the action. It could already look like a bad episode of Jerry Springer, you know, screaming and hair-pulling.

I swear the stairs aren't wide enough for someone as big as me, but I make my way down. I hear an unfamiliar voice, a female voice.

"I don't want to hear your damned excuses! I saved his

life, and I came to get a damn thank you, so either you go get him or I'll go up there myself!"

Ooh, she's certainly as feisty as she was at the bar and in my fantasies.

The room went quiet once everyone saw me coming down the stairs, including her. She did not look happy.

Cheetah can barely contain his amusement. "Uhhh Cupid, you got a visitor." They empty the room and it's me and her. I take my seat in the recliner as she stands there, arms crossed.

I couldn't help but notice her outfit of choice. She wore a sheer white tank top and a cute pink bra with little flowers on it. Like I said, it was a very sheer top. I swear I can see her nipples poking out... or maybe I'm optimistic. She finished the outfit by wearing bleached blue jean cutoff shorts that showed off her sculpted tan legs, small waist, and belly button.

I know she's talking cause she's waving her arms and flailing about like a fish out of water, but I'm having a hard time focusing. I shake my head and am transported back into the present.

"I'm sorry. What did you say?"

She's clearly irritated that I zoned out and didn't hear a word she said.

"What the hell, did you sustain brain damage in that fight? Ya hard of hearing?!"

Now she was pushing my buttons. I don't appreciate being yelled at in my own place. It's disrespectful and I don't do well with disrespect.

I stood up so she could see me tower over her and get some sense. I see her swallow hard as she takes me all in. I must be one hell of a sight in my black silk boxers. I have to will myself to not get a boner staring at her tits from this angle.

I caught the hitch in her breath, but she stiffened up. "I'm here for the thank you that you owe me for saving your life! It's the least you could say!"

Like I said, feisty.

"Kitten, you've got balls *and* claws coming in here demanding I give you *anything*. There will be no thanking you for sticking your nose in my business where it didn't belong. So, you can be on your way."

I gestured towards the door, and she reeled as if I smacked her in the face. She inhaled before she approached me with fire in her eyes. Her tiny figure stood against mine with her finger poking my chest.

"You listen here, buddy, there is a thing called gratitude for someone saving your sorry ass life and decent human beings usually say thank you, but what did I expect from a greasy, low-life miscreant like you! So, you're goddamned welcome for saving your miserable life and you can fuck off for all I care!"

She spins on her heel and slams the door on her way out. How did she even get here?

There were a million other questions I had, but the one burning my soul was why I had such a painful erection after our encounter.

Shit.

I better get upstairs before they rag on me and my "arrow."

What are you doing to me, kitten?

Lyric

That motherfucker! That... that tall... blonde... handsome bastard! The nerve of him and that strong heaving chest covered in tattoos and delicious piercings. I bet he gets off when tugged on during sex. And those boxers that covered absolutely nothing. I saw everything. The size of it almost made me forget why I was there. I wasn't blind to the fact that he definitely had the equipment for a screaming good time.

Focus, Lyric! Don't forget how condescending he was towards you!

I shouldn't have gone there. I should've let him get shot. What do I care? But I couldn't stand there! Whatever, screw him, I'm going into work! I got there about an hour early and wanted to make sure everything was immaculate to make up for my actions yesterday.

"Hey, Lyric."

"Hey, Dave. Listen, I'm really sorry about my part in what happened yesterday. I didn't mean to..." I look up to our new sunroof, praying it doesn't rain.

He holds his hand up. "Don't worry, I'm going up there to patch it up. This is a bar and brawls happen all the time. Wasn't the first and won't be the last. I'm glad you weren't hurt. You've only been here a couple of months, but I've been here the whole miserable 42 years of my life. The short story is the Aces have been the reigning club for years. Nothing bad about them. They look mean and ominous, but overall, good guys. Johnny's 'gang', though, are all bad apples. Nothing good can come from them."

He stocks the register with bills for the day, always the same amount, $150, so he can calculate profit by the end of the shift. I make sure the bar is fully stocked and the cans are on ice. We work our routines in comfortable silence.

"So, tell me more about them, the Aces." I couldn't help it; I was dying to know.

He chuckles, shaking his head. "Well, Jackal is the leader of all those knuckleheads. He wasn't here yesterday, but you'd know who he was. He founded the chapter long ago alongside his beautiful wife, Paige. They took in any troubled soul who needed it. Paige was an angel on Earth, but a few years back, cancer took her from this world to the next. He took it pretty hard, as expected. We didn't see the gang for almost two months as they nursed him back to life. What he is now is a shell of his former self, but he still has his boys and that keeps him going. Each fella has their story of how they came to be an Ace, each one unique. Their clubhouse isn't too far from here off route..."

"Oh, I know where it is. I was there this morning." I blurted out while cleaning the bar glasses, then I froze. I felt my ears heat up because I knew I was in for a tongue lashing.

Dave turned and looked at me, clearly shocked. "Why on Earth would you go there?"

I shrugged, feeling scolded. "I... I felt I deserved a damn thank you for saving his life! It's the decent thing to say. Is *thank you* so hard?"

Dave leans against the bar and sighs. I could see the concern in his eyes, like a dad has with his daughter. "Lyric, listen to me. These are biker boys with no feeling or remorse. They're known for using girls and tossing them aside. They even have designated girls for sex only. You're a nice, smart, pretty girl. I don't want to see you get hurt. Just be careful, please."

I roll my eyes. I'm no damsel in distress and he, for fuck sure, wasn't no Romeo. I wanted what's due, that's all. I wasn't hoping he would take me on top of that bar, rip every article of clothing from my body, and then his strong arms wrap around my waist as he pounds into me...

Whoa! Where did that come from?! Settle down, woman.

I nod to ease his mind as I check the taps. A few were low and dispensing foam. I write all the names to go back into the closet and swap them out. It's going to be a long day.

Cupid

After yanking it twice, I got dressed and met the guys downstairs.

Jackal was puffing away his Macanudo robusto in his cognac leather recliner, listening to Digi prattle on about something undoubtedly computer related. He knew he wouldn't understand a word Digi said, but Prez had a soft spot for Digi since he was the one to find him wandering aimlessly around downtown.

Someone tossed him out of a van outside of town, and he walked the rest of the way in, leaving him dehydrated and delirious. He believes his hacker group grew to fear his abilities and needed to get rid of him before someone dangerous came after them. Their loss was our gain.

Digi had surveillance on the whole town. He was prospering under Prez's watchful eye. I like to think of him as my baby brother. He follows me around from time to time, seeking advice.

I head behind the bar and pour myself a stiff shot of rum, as if I hadn't been stiff enough.

I was alone with my thoughts until, "Hey Cupid, did you get your rocks off with your fiery visitor? Girlie has some claws, probably scratched you up good, huh?"

"Shut up, Cheetah. She came in yelling at me for not thanking her and then left. She had some nerve expecting me to say thank you."

I take a sip as Jackal huffs.

Oh, here comes the wisdom.

"Now, I didn't witness what happened at the bar, but that little firecracker stood tall against me and the fellas when she came banging on the door this morning. She was not backing down. I'd reconsider that hardcore hatred and really get to know her. I mean, she *did* save your life."

What the hell is going on here? If he thinks I'm just going to crack under the pressure of some smart-mouthed tart, he's got another thing coming.

I grunt as my response, then throw back the rest of my drink.

It'll be a cold day in hell...

"I know you hear me, but I won't push it. We still have to settle this mess with Johnny. Club, Knox, you go this time. I drew up another treaty. Tell him there is no need for retaliation or war. Go, now!"

Club and Knox do what Prez says and make their way to Johnny's lair or maybe back to the bar. I assume scumbags gather in low-lying places.

Hope this works because I don't know what I will do the next time we cross paths. I'm sick of dealing with everyone else's problems.

Flashback

Well, it didn't last long with Mr. Wellington. I remember the screaming from their last argument. I was hiding around the corner, keeping myself from knocking his teeth down his throat. I had to let this play out.

"All I ever wanted was for us to be a family, Carey! You said when you came back that's what you wanted, too! All you've done is lie!"

He ran his hands roughly through his hair, his hand on his hip as he paced. "I have a life in California where I'm rich and virile. More women than I could ever handle! I don't need this! You didn't even do what you were supposed to? You didn't tell him. Why should I stick around? My life is way more important there than in this run down town...so goodbye, Diane."

She lurched like she took a bullet and reached out for him, but he quickly got out of her grasp.

"Carey, wait! Carey!"

I watch that bastard walk right past me and out the door. He left me with a hysterically crying mother. At my touch, she tried to pull herself together, but it was no use. She wailed as if someone had died. The fact is, someone had. It was her.

This was by far her worst breakup, I guess because they had history, but that must have been long before I was born because I don't have any recollection of the fucker before this time around.

My knuckles rap softly against the worn wood of Mom's door; the silence that follows is heavy, a suffocating blanket. I know she won't answer—the familiar scent of stale grief and self-pity hangs in the air, thick and cloying. This time, the darkness feels colder, deeper; a palpable weight pressing down.

Days turned into weeks. She grew weaker. One day, she had a 104° fever. I rushed her to the emergency room. They immediately put her on a stretcher and worked to lower her temperature. I spoke with her doctor, requesting a psychiatric evaluation and commitment, if deemed necessary. I only hoped to salvage what remained of my mother's well-being. He agreed, and her psychiatrist recommended inpatient treatment for her bipolar disorder and other mental health concerns.

I fended for myself for the next three weeks. It wasn't easy. I ate very little and stayed home, waiting for the call. Finally, one day it came.

My mom was well enough to come home.

She waited outside of the hospital for me in the issued gown, her belongings in a plastic bag. When our eyes met, I knew she hadn't forgiven me, and I wasn't sure she ever would.

She spent the next two days in silence, sitting on the patio overlooking the backyard and a small lake. She'd just watch the day go by and when I came to check on her, she'd just take her blanket and go to her room without a word towards me. I'd bring her food and eventually she'd eat it. It was a small but significant sign she was getting better, even if she was shutting me out.

I was napping on the couch a week later when she woke me. "You know, you're the only constant in my life. The only man to love me genuinely. I know having me committed was hard, and I never blamed you. You were trying to save what's left of me. I should only be so appreciative that my son did that for me."

I sat up and faced her. She looked like her old self, in her vintage calico 6os dress, her hair in a chignon and she even put on her signature berry devilish lipstick. She told me the color once, so if she ever ran out, I would know what to get.

She looked like my mom again, but I was highly skeptical...
Just how long would this last?
Flashback end

Lyric

It's been almost a week since the bar fight fiasco. Another day, another dollar in this rat trap.

Okay, I should really stop trashing the place. It's a good gig just with not so great customers.

I sigh as I clear the mess that table three left before I hear a strained cough behind me.

"Well, well, well... look who it is. I think you owe me an apology, bitch. I don't take kindly to you assaulting me like that. I haven't done anything to you yet. You're going to pay for this."

Before I can get away from the threatening voice, I'm spun around to face the vengeful eyes of Johnny. He's got a bandage wrapped around his head that had a bit of blood seeping through.

I didn't think I hit him that hard, but the pained look, flickering between his rage, told a different story. Guess I had built up all this rage and aggression. Screw him, he deserved much worse.

He was so close it was uncomfortable. I could see the residue from his last hit and that made him dangerous, with fresh drugs coursing through his veins. He would show no remorse.

"So, you want to be a whore to the Aces, huh? Well, I'll make sure I return the damaged goods to them as soon as I'm done making you pay."

I looked frantically for Dave but he's nowhere to be found, only Johnny's cronies. My heart hammers a frantic rhythm against my ribs, a trapped bird desperate for escape. The air tastes metallic, a bitter tang accompanying the hot, prickly tears welling in my eyes. My vision blurs momentarily, a frantic scan of the room, searching for a lifeline, a friendly face, anyone!

"No one's going to rescue you, slut. Now, I believe you owe me an apology. Oh, and so much more..." He licked his lips and rubbed his hands together.

Oh god, oh god, oh god! I don't know what to do! I have to fight back, or he'll hurt me. Either way, I can't make it easy for him. I'd rather die first!

His whiskey scented breath on my ear. "I won't ask again, slut..." He rasps and then pulls back to gauge my reaction, which is pure fear. I couldn't even squeak out an answer; the silence was deafening. Then, I felt the sharp sting of his hand across my face, a searing heat followed by throbbing pain. I stumbled, the rough wood of the bar digging into my back as I clutched my face, the taste of blood metallic and acrid. Shock and horror solidified into a cold, clammy dread.

He wasn't done.

"If you won't *give* me an apology, then I'll just have to *take* that, too."

That threat causes me to go back behind the bar. Each step back, he takes a step forward. In fear, I throw the first bottle I can get my hands on, but he deflects it. It bounces and slides off the counter before hitting the floor. He and his buddies laugh.

"Let's see how strong that gag reflex is. I'll go first, then you can all get a turn after."

I bolted toward the other end of the bar, but a searing

pain shot through my scalp as someone yanked my hair. Another brutal slap sent me sprawling to my knees. The tears fall in my weakened and vulnerable state, and my lip quivers.

"Mmm... can't wait to feel those pretty lips rub all over this hard dick. Open up, sweetheart..."

Helplessness choked me as I sobbed, my pleas lost in the suffocating horror of the moment. I see his friends watching and egging him on to hurt me... to violate me. I just hoped it would end quickly.

What did I do to deserve this? I shut my eyes and accept my fate.

"HEY! HEY, JUST WHAT THE FUCK ARE YOU DOING TO HER?! YOU MOTHERFUCKERS!"

A clash of shouts pierces the air, the sharp crackle of voices making my head spin as I watch them turn, faces contorted in anger. A wave of icy terror washes over me, stealing my breath as the world blurs. The dull thud of fists meeting flesh, a sickening rhythm, fills my ears before the darkness claims me.

Cupid

It was a nice breezy day outside, so I tended to my cherry red beauty, my Harley Davidson deluxe. I keep her well maintained. She's my baby, my escape.

She's taken me far and wide along the countryside, from coast to coast. Nothing like the freedom of having your boots up doing 85 down the highway.

It's been a while since I've taken a decent ride, even a quick one. Club business keeps us grounded here. One day, I'll take off and go to California to see the ocean again.

Nothing was more serene than the breeze that came off the waves of the ocean.

I heard a rumbling and looked up to see rain clouds approaching, so I wheeled her into the garage after the badass wax job I just gave her.

I hear Club and Knox's cruisers coming up the driveway, but stop short of the barn, like they were in front of the house instead. Weird.

"You got her? Well, get her in the house! I'll find every-one. Hey! Aces emergency meeting, living room, now!" I hear Club yell toward the garage.

Christ almighty, now what? I assume it didn't go well at the meeting. I cover my beauty and stomp towards the front door. As I walk in, I see the fellas gathered in front of the couch. They're whispering and I hear my name come up.

"Cupid's going to fucking flip! Scorched Earth, man. We gotta reveal this delicately."

What did I do?

I was the last to come in. My heavy boots caused everyone to turn around.

Jackal turns to intercept me. "Hey Cupid, let me talk to you for a moment over here." Jackal points to the far corner of the room near the door and away from the commotion. That can't be good. I follow, and he keeps my focus away from the group.

Jackal turned around, my back to the group, as he watched me for a moment. I saw the worry in his eyes; he never hid his emotions anymore.

"Look, I don't need you to go nuclear, but... there was... an incident at the bar today with Johnny. He, uh, he cornered that little lady behind the bar and..." He took a deep breath, "he was going to assault her for helping you. If

Club and Knox hadn't been there, I don't know how bad it would have been, but I have to be honest, she suffered some physical injuries from him. They brought her here, and I want you to be prepared."

He glanced down; the stark white of my knuckles mirrored the fury that burned within me, a taut spring ready to snap. As soon as he said "her" my blood was boiling.

To threaten a woman with physical assault was one of my no-going-back deals. I'd go to jail, bathed in the blood of any bastard who harmed a woman or child.

Jackal noticed my anger induced trance, and snapped me out of it. "Cupid, you need to be calm; she's blacked out and hasn't regained consciousness yet. She needs to see a familiar face when she awakens. I know she'll be frightened and reliving the trauma. Be her comfort. Can you do that?" He clutched my shoulders so I could focus on his face and what he was saying, not fixate on my increasing rage. I could only nod.

If he wasn't a dead man before, he definitely was now. The various ways I wanted to torture and kill that fucker were uncontrollably rampant in my mind, but I had to focus. My chest burned with a furious heat as I faced her laying on the couch, my breaths ragged and shallow with uncontrolled rage.

A clear as day, bright red handprint across her face and a cut above her eyebrow.

I'll slice his dick off, shove it down his fucking throat, and then stomp on his windpipe.

As my darkness actively conjured up a torture to-do list, I gazed at her. She was still out cold when I knelt in front of her. Her hair covers part of her face but not the handprint. Her face was swollen, and I can't help but feel the bruise, which felt warm to the touch. She flinches and stirs a bit. Her eyes clamp shut like she was reliving the incident. I brush her hair from her face.

"Oh, kitten..."

I pick her up, maneuver up the stairs, and place her in my bed. Removing her shoes and socks. I sit in the recliner next to my bed and watch an angel sleep.

What have I gotten her mixed up in?

Lyric

I'm struggling to get away from that druggie bastard. He wants to hurt me; he wants to violate me and teach me a lesson, but I won't stop fighting. He'll never win! I'd rather die first! I want to scream but it's muffled, though in my mind it sounds like a thousand banshees.

I have to get away! I have to get free from him!

"Ahhhhh! Get away! Don't touch me, you son of a..."

"Hey, hey, hey kitten, wake up!"

My eyes shoot open, but it's pitch black, and I don't know who is talking to me. My eyes haven't adjusted.

Oh god, did Johnny kidnap me and is now holding me hostage? I got to get out! I got to get out! I...

Before I could bolt, the lights turned on and I'm face to face with Tarzan. My Tarzan. I have never been so relieved to see his stupid, arrogant face.

A wave of emotion came crashing over. I didn't think. I just jumped into his arms and cried. I wanted to be held, to feel safe.

Cupid

She pounced right into my lap and cried. She had to be terrified after today's incident. She's not going back. I'll be damned. I'll take her to grab some items from her place, but I will not leave her alone. This is my fault.

She's sniffling, but finally comfortably asleep. Subconsciously, she's rubbing her inner thigh, then she whimpers. It's not one of fear, but one of lust.

"I need you... please..." I watch her hand slide further inward. I know the softness and warmth between a woman's legs. She probably does that out of habit. It's innocent, I tell myself.

But then, I watched this petite beauty's hand slip underneath her leggings and underwear as she shifted her focus to pleasure. Right there in my lap. I imagined she was dripping wet as she stroked herself, concentrating on her sensitive clit. Her little gasps and moans were mind-blowingly sexy. She started panting, and my arrow couldn't be stiffer. I'd give anything to ease the deep throbbing. All I had to do was shift her so I could pull my dick out, stroke myself until we both came.

No. She had experienced something so traumatic. This was not the time to indulge in fantasies. It was selfish.

"Mmm, right there..." Her sleep talking interrupted my thoughts.

I'm conflicted. Do I stop her or let her finish?

She's been through enough and I just watch. If I move, I'll wake her and that'll be awkward enough.

Her other hand slides up, slipping under the t-shirt I put her in, to caress her breast and it's obvious the tempo changes with her lower hand, as her fingers work rapidly to bring her to climax.

Her mix of whimpering and moaning is driving me wild. Fuck, my jeans are pinching my dick against my thigh.

"Mmm...so close...Cupid, please."

Holy shit!

She just moaned my name! That little minx was getting off to the thought of me.

Fuck, that's hot.

Her breathing picks up as she physically shakes from her orgasm and comes all over her fingers. She sighs before she calms back down to a deeper slumber. Her hand now laid on my chest. I wanted to lick her fingers clean, tasting her essence.

This is by far the most painful erection I've ever had, as I just watched this girl come while moaning my name. I placed her gently on my bed and went to take a shower, where I let my imagination run wild.

I couldn't jerk off fast enough. My body shuddered, my knees buckled, and I bit my tongue as it brought me to my knees. This was my quickest orgasm to date. She worked me up, watching her writhe on top of me, spilling her orgasm all over her hand.

I change into a t-shirt and shorts before I lay down and pull her in. I don't know why this feels right when I don't even let the bunnies rest after a good fuck session, but she was different. She buries her face into my neck, and I play in her hair until I fall asleep.

Lyric

I finally opened my eyes from today's nightmare to realize it's nighttime and nothing looks familiar, not the walls, the decor or the layout I could see as my eyes adjusted. My stomach sank to the realization, this isn't my place!

My breathing picked up even more when I realized that someone was holding me. In a panic, I turn around, create space, and shove as hard as I could to get away.

I heard the man yelp and body fall to the floor. "Ahh, what the hell?! Why'd you push me off the bed? Remember earlier? I told you that you're safe with me." Then he groaned.

That wasn't Johnny's voice. It wasn't cold or sinister.

Then a lamp turns on and I instantly remember what happened before I fell asleep. I was crying...in his arms. He must have placed me on his bed and was... holding me so that I knew I was safe. I am so embarrassed!

"Oh gosh, I am so sorry! I panicked again. I must have had another nightmare! I'm... I'm sorry, Cupid."

He sighs, defeated. "Call me Aleister, please."

I nod as I pull the blanket back. "Will you get back in bed, please, Aleister?"

Cupid

Her eyes scream to be comforted, and I oblige. I lay flat on my back, reach over, and turn off the lamp. The room sits peacefully still. Suddenly, she turns and lays half her body on my chest and leg. I put my hands behind my head to avoid any accidental touch.

I shift a bit. "You know, you never told me your name after you yelled at me, told me to fuck off, and stormed out of here." Even in the dark, I could feel her glare from here. Well, that was my failed attempt at lightening the mood.

She scoffed. "And you never thanked me for saving your life. Guess we're even then."

There's an awkward silence. Then she sighs, her soft body relaxing even more into me. "It's Lyric."

Her name was Lyric, and she was the sweetest melody. Fuck! I take a deep breath as she places her hand on my chest. I sigh before conceding, gritting my teeth. "Thank you for saving me."

"See, was that so difficult? Had you done it earlier, I

wouldn't have called you all those names and told you to fuck off."

"I'm sure."

She giggles, and it sounds like honey to a bee.

I have no idea what I just said...it sounded like music to my ears.

I didn't want to ruin the mood, but I needed to know. I shifted, but her body followed mine.

"Tell me what happened."

A shudder racked her body, and I put my arm over her for comfort.

"I-I don't know. Look, one minute I was cleaning tables and the next they were surrounding me. He was so threatening. He said he would... would hurt me. I was so scared he was going to succeed. Nobody was there to help me until your brothers came." She shook her head against me. "I can't go back! I won't. He called me the Aces whore, like I was an object."

I had to clench my fist that rested on my leg several times to dissipate my growing rage. She was no whore, and didn't deserve to be threatened by that crackhead lunatic. I don't care what Jackal says. If it's a war he wants, a war he fucking gets!

I sigh as she is silent again.

"Still awake?" I ask curiously.

She nods her head and traces circles on my chest. She's getting dangerously close to my piercings and I might shoot up like a fire hose on full blast. Her leg would feel it instantly. I was already on edge. I had watched her masturbate and moan my name. It sounded so delicious, too. I have to force myself not to think about it.

Then she brushes against my nipple piercing, and I gasp.

"Sorry." She whispered, her fingers moving to a safer area.

"It's okay, it's just an erogenous zone."

Why did I just say that?!

She chuckles and places her hand on her own hip. For some strange reason, I miss the heat of her finger circling my chest, temptingly teasing me as she twirls her thoughts and emotions all over me.

"Can I ask you something personal?" She interrupts my daydreaming.

"Shoot." I answer against my better judgment.

"What do you have against love?"

I scoff. "Love never did me any good. It's a weak emotion, for suckers and saps. Completely unnecessary. I don't need it to live. I've done just fine without it."

"You don't love anyone? What about your mom or dad?"

"I didn't know the bastard, but yes, I loved my mother, but she's dead now and she died from love. Her heartbreak killed her. I have no use for love, if that's what it does."

My grunt, intended to end the conversation, seemed to work, as she quieted and I could hear her gentle snoring.

Thank goodness. I tilted my head down to meet the top of her head and drifted off.

In the wee hours of the morning, Digi texted all of us the gruesome details and the footage. It was difficult to watch as they tied and gagged Dave to his office chair. He tried to shout and struggle. Johnny watched him while attaching the suppressor before shooting him four times, two to the kneecaps, heart, and then head.

I lost it and went into my closet and punched the wall several times, which was a mistake because it was concrete, not drywall, but it was too late. It was in rapid succession until I stopped. Probably not the smartest idea, but I didn't want to startle her.

I try to calm my breathing when I hear her groan; I hope I didn't wake her, but now I have to tell her.

I walk toward the bathroom and see her touching her face. It probably hurts. I grab the aspirin, a glass of water, and hand it to her. She keeps her eyes closed while trying to take the pills. It must be the sun, so I shut the curtains, and she sighs in relief.

She is stunning in the morning light, her hair tousled about and her eyes sparkle. I can't deny her beauty, but I have to dial it back and break the bad news.

Lyric

I wake up in searing pain; a sharp, throbbing ache stabs my left cheek where Johnny hit me. A groan escapes my lips. Harsh sunlight, a blinding white glare from the window, intensifies the agony.

"Morning darlin', here I knew you'd be sore."

He hands me two aspirin and a glass of water. I attempted to take the pills with my eyes closed. Aleister pulls the curtains and I sigh in relief. I needed my wits if I was going to face the bar again.

He sits on the edge of the bed. I look down at his hands and realize there are cuts and scratches all over them and he's bleeding!

"Oh my gosh, you're hurt! What happened? Did Johnny come here?"

He looks down and realizes that I noticed, and he

quickly stands up and steps back. "Listen, Lyric, there's been a discovery, and it's not good news."

He looks away but focuses back on me when I get up to take his hands and survey the damage. I get a warm, wet towel to clean the cuts. I try to be incredibly careful.

He hisses, "I'm sorry to tell you this, but your boss is dead. Looks like they attacked him in his office before getting to you. Johnny knew Dave would've protected you with his life, and he did. If they had gotten to you sooner..." His jaw clenches, trying not to think about what could have been.

My hands are shaking so badly I can't even hold the washcloth. Hot tears streamed down my face, blurring my vision as the crushing weight of my guilt settled in; the sweetest man I knew was gone, and it was all my fault.

I don't know when it happened, but suddenly, I felt his arms around me, his heartbeat echoing in my ears. His comfort helps me grieve the loss of the only man I knew in this place.

I feel so weak, so helpless, but I can't let it consume me.

After I broke the news, I watched her as she quietly went and got dressed in the hallway bathroom. She comes down to breakfast, but it's just the two of us since everyone has already eaten and is now outside tending to their bikes.

She looked so heartbroken. "Listen, I know it's been a rough 24 hours. I want you to stay here until we can get more information, especially with Johnny still roaming free. Let me protect you." She looks up and I can see the tears welling in her eyes. She's replaying the details of Dave's death. Thank god she didn't ask to see the footage, but I also didn't tell her about it. Dave was a hero and died trying to keep Johnny from hurting her.

She focuses on the food in front of her, pushing the

oatmeal around the bowl. After a few tiny bites, she quietly washes the dishes. I tell her we're going to her place to grab some things. She hops on my bike behind me and we take a brief ride to her apartment.

It's part of the town I am not that familiar with. Seedy is the best way to describe it. The building was worn down and rough looking, with no security measures for their tenants. I wasn't even sure it had working utilities until I stepped into her apartment and she flipped on the lights. It's a cracker box. I think my closet is bigger than this. She crouches down on this dingy mustard yellow carpet to grab a bag from under her bed. I pray it is close to the original color and not tinted from years of neglect. She looks at me wide eyed. I can see she's trying to hold back the tears.

"Will, will I ever come back here?"

I shake my head. "It's too dangerous. He'll come for you if he hasn't already staked the place out to attack. You'll stay with me and I won't take no for an answer. Actually, I'm not asking, Lyric."

She did not like that last statement as she went from wide eyed to pissed in a few seconds.

Easy there, "hero." I don't appreciate your possessive attitude. I belong to no one, so if this is how you're going to be, I can sleep on the couch. Or I'm sure one of your friends wouldn't mind a guest in their bed.

She stomped toward her closet, muttering under her breath. I wasn't one for mixed signals, but I felt possessive, especially after her threat to sleep elsewhere. I'd break their jaw, brothers or not!

I nervously ran my fingers through my hair and paced the tiny space, covering it in four strides. I was deep in my thoughts when she came back out.

She paused. "What the hell are you doing? Weirdo..."

Her tossing her things into the bag, and occasional glances in my direction, caught my attention. What do I say to her?

"Nothing, nothing..."

She huffs and rolls her eyes. Without further comment, she locked up, and we went back to my bike. "I need to go to the bar." I was about to deny her, but she held her hand up. "Before you spout some bullshit of why it's dangerous or blah blah blah, I need to access the safe and take the money and his documents. Besides...you'll be right behind me."

She smiled slyly, put her bag on the bike, and walked to the bar a short distance away. I follow her and the sway in her hips, the curve of her ass, and the...

"Hey, Cupid, keep your eyes on your arrow, okay?"

Busted.

Oh kitten, if you only knew the underlying connotation to that.

Lyric

I feel his gaze like burning lasers on my ass. To be a little mischievous, I exaggerate the sway of my hips. I chuckle to myself, then turn to meet his eyes.

"Hey, Cupid, keep your eyes on your arrow, okay?"

I turn back and laugh as I hear him grumble. He's adorable, but I still wonder what caused his aversion to love? Or who?

We reached the heavy saloon doors, the yellow caution tape stark against the dark wood. A metallic tang hung in the air, mixed with the faint scent of stale beer. My throat tightened, a dry swallow catching as I replayed what probably happened and how he felt: the panic, the bone-deep help-lessness, the searing pain.

What hurt worse is that I knew his final thoughts were about me and my safety.

I can't move.

I hear his heavy boot steps stop right behind me and my breath stutters. His hands grip my arms and then he side steps and goes in first, pulling the tape down.

The shudder of the door startles me and I push forward, not wanting to be too far from him.

Boy, his club brothers did a number to this place when they pummeled Johnny and his lackeys. Broken chairs and bottles sprawled on the floor. I think someone smashed some-one's head against the mirror by the bar.

"Hey..." I jumped, not realizing Aleister was behind me. I felt his body heat radiating over mine.

"Huh?"

"The office." I knew he was trying to keep this trip short to avoid additional emotional damage.

My feet finally carry me toward the back. I try to brace myself, but then he grabs my arm, turning me to face him. This is where he died, where he bled and took his last breath. Where his last words were trying to warn me.

"Maybe I should go first. I heard it wasn't a pretty sight."

That got my heart racing and breathing erratic. Could I handle that? I needed to keep his documents and save the bar! It's the least I could do for the man who died trying to save me.

Meanwhile, Aleister's gazing into my eyes as a million thoughts run through. I stand straighter and square my shoulders. "I, uh, I can do it."

I open the door, and the brevity of the situation hits me

hard as I look around. He struggled and fought until they overpowered him. The signs were all over his office with strewn papers and turned over furniture, but I was grateful they cleaned up the blood.

I closed my eyes and took a deep breath. After proving my worth, Dan trusted me with the combination to the safe. I was the only other person who had access.

With a turn of the dial, the tumblers clicked into place one by one, and with a final click, the door opened before me. I pull the green utility box and shut it.

"Okay, let's get out of here, please."

He gestures toward the box. "We have a blowtorch to open that, if you need it." I pull a chain from around my collar. "Don't worry, he gave me a key."

I shut the door and turned off the lights, wondering if I'll ever return.

Cupid

With her bag resting securely across my lap, and her small hands gripping my waist tightly, we made our way back to the clubhouse. I park, put the kickstand into position, and grab her bag, turning to her.

"Listen, this is not a power struggle. I need you to stay in my room, not in the living room or anywhere else. I want you to be safe."

This wasn't establishing dominance or maybe it was, but she was a firecracker and I had to be crystal clear.

It seemed as if she was about to unleash a fiery reply, but then her eyes became calm and gentle, and a simple nod was all the response she offered. I was stunned.

Lyric

I am completely drained of any energy to engage in conflict or put up a fight, as my life takes an overwhelmingly negative turn, deteriorating from bad to utterly catastrophic. I'm mentally exhausted and just wanted to sleep.

I walk in and the men are laughing and drinking... until they see me. They straighten up really quick, like a bunch of choirboys caught red-handed with daddy's secret porno stash.

I give a small smile. "Uh, hi. I guess I should introduce myself since you all saved my life. I'm Lyric."

A tall older man with a gray beard stepped forward. This was definitely their leader. He shook my hand with a firm grip.

"I'm Jackal, President of the Black Aces and this is Cheetah, Digi, Club, Knox, and Blondie there. Of course, you know Cupid."

I see him practically blocking the doorway with my bag on his shoulder. I turned back. "Yup, very aware."

He just winks. Sexy bastard...

"Have a seat, Lyric. Would you like a drink?"

"No, thank you, but I could use a meal?"

Club hops up, "I'll get the grill going and Digi can help make the sides." Digi follows him into the kitchen.

"Club is almost a master chef so you are in for one helluva meal." Blondie says while crafting some sort of drink.

"I look forward to it. I think that gives me some time. Is it okay if I go lie down?"

Cup-, I mean Aleister moves forward with my bag.

"Come on, I'll get you settled."

I follow him up the stairs. I open the familiar door and relent as I pull off my shirt and plop down on the bed, face down. It didn't even register because I like to sleep shirtless, sometimes less. I gasp as I realize what I had done, but he was already in the room and I was facing him in my sheer lacy black bra. I forgot just how see through it was. It was too late by then.

Cupid

My mouth went dry, just from the sight of her back's gentle curve, her skin so soft it looked like warm silk. A tiny, charming tattoo peeked from her right shoulder. Then, she turned, the scent of her perfume, a light floral, drifting to me.

Fuck me sideways, my eyes beelined to her perky tawny nipples in that sheer black bra.

Nice.

I tugged at my beard and licked my lips without thinking. To break the stare, I set her bag down while she turned around, laid on the bed, and crossed her legs in the air.

"Sorry, it's a habit." She squeaks out as she rests her head on her crossed arms.

"No worries. I'll come back when the food is done. Get some rest."

Lyric

He shuts the door behind him, and I turn to lie on my back. I spread my legs wide and focus intensely on pleasuring my throbbing clit.

Oh, fuck. I can't help myself!

My fingers, slick with desire, move in and out with practiced ease. A soft coo escapes my lips. "Ohhh yes..." The rough assault on my nipples sends delicious twinges of pain shooting through me. A delightful shiver runs down my spine, raising goosebumps on my skin. I moan his name, a low, guttural sound, lost in the pleasure of self care.

"Oh, Aleister...it feels so good. I'm so close. Please."

My pace quickened; the knot that formed unraveled rapidly. I slapped my hand across my mouth, muffling a scream into my palm as tremors racked my body. Gasping for breath, I rolled over, collapsing into a restless slumber. Until I hear a squeak...

Cupid

Fuck me and all that is holy.

I knew I should go, but a strange compulsion held me captive, and the next moment, her desperate gasps and whimpers cut through the quiet.

She can't be! Could she? I wonder how often she does that, knowingly and unknowingly.

My dick shot up so fast I needed to will it away before I went downstairs. That's all I needed was another reason for them to rag on me.

But my mind wandered to what I would do. I would burst in, knocking the door off the frame, and take her. Not a quick conquest either, but a slow, sensual undoing. To hear her gasps and moans, a symphony of pleasure echoing in the air, thick with the scent of her perfume and arousal. To taste her sweetness, the essence of her climax spilling over my lips. Then, the greedy slam of my body into her warm, wet pussy, a friction that ignites us both.

I recognized this time she called me by my God-given

name. The name Aleister never sounded so sweet coming from her lips. Hearing nothing else, I assume she orgasmed herself to sleep.

Quietly tiptoeing down the hall, my boots suddenly squeaked on the wood. I crossed my fingers that she was fast asleep and didn't notice.

Lyric

Holy fucking shit!

He was still outside of the door when I... took care of myself. He heard me call his name! I can never face him again. I have no choice but to starve up here.

An hour, and no sleep later, there's a light knock.

"I'm awake." I say, reluctantly sitting up.

Luckily, it's Digi. He's so adorable and the baby of the group, no older than 20 or 21. He's tall and scrawny, with sandy brown hair and wireless glasses. If I had another brother, I'd think he'd look like him. He's looking down instead of looking at me. I can still see the blush forming on his cheek.

"Din-dinner is ready. I mean, if you're hungry."

So sweet!

"Thank you, Digi, I'll be right down."

Well, time to face the music and look right into the eyes of the man I masturbated to who definitely heard me.

I changed into a flowy floral print dress; I almost went without underwear, but I'd slide right off my seat. Finally, I clip my hair up, slip on my sandals, and go downstairs.

Picture this: a standard-sized table, seven enormous guys squeezed around it, somehow trying to look perfectly at home when they actually looked super uncomfortable. It caused me to laugh hysterically.

They all look at me like I'm crazy while I'm laughing.

"Guys, guys, you don't have to pretend to eat like this just because a lady is here. It's ok to be yourselves. I insist, fellas."

It was a collective group sigh, as they got up and moved to their normal eating positions in the living room and at the bar and chowed down.

I shake my head as I go into the kitchen and search for plates. A pair of large tattooed hands opens a cabinet and hand me a delicate plate. I look up to Aleister staring down at me.

"T-thank you." I followed his stare to the low cut of my dress. He was tall, so he had a bird's-eye view. A smirk plays on my lips as I carefully take my plate to the kitchen island. He watches as I fix my plate.

"What are you, plate monitor?"

His chuckle broke the tension, and I felt a rush of warmth between my legs. "Just making sure you don't need to reach anything else high up."

Oh, ha ha, a short joke.

I looked at him and rolled my eyes. "Don't you need to eat? Sounds like the wolf pack is starving. Do you guys only eat once a day?"

He grunts. "We eat plenty, just a group of hungry bikers always ready to...eat." A shiver shot up my spine as I stiffened, trying to not make it obvious.

"Uh-huh." I take my plate into the living room and sit on the sofa next to Jackal in his leather chair.

Cupid plops down beside me, plate in hand, in the only seat left.

Subtle guys, real subtle.

I shake my head. I saw him sneak a glance before going back to his food.

Just as I was chatting, three girls walked in. They are wearing short skirts and skimpy tops that accentuate their busts, but not very well.

I knew enough about motorcycle clubs to know patch pussy when I saw it. No offense intended. ***insert eye roll***

They're loud and talkative, but that all stops when three pairs of eyes fixate on me, and I become the subject of their collective, intense scrutiny.

Here we go people...

This overly proportionate blonde waves her cheap red press-on nail in my direction. "Ummm, who is she?!"

Good lord, if they were her real friends, they'd tell her she reeked of hooker.

She sneered at me. Her lip curled up in disgust.

Don't try me bleach blonde bimbo.

I'm sure my face said it all, but Cupid tucked his arm around me and slid me towards him, never saying a word. It was all interpretation.

Ok, I'll play along. I cross my legs toward him and smile.

"That's Lyric, s-she's Cupid's girl." Digi stuttered out and I swear her eyes were so wide they could have fallen out.

Cupid didn't deny the statement. Is that what he wanted? AM I his girl? We can't even hold a proper conversation without a blowout pissing match. I'll figure that out later. She was livid. She clearly likes him, but club bunnies are supposed to be temporary.

My thoughts were interrupted by her angry approach; she stopped before him, arms crossed, clearly waiting for a response, yet his continued silence only pissed her off even more.

"So instead of hittin' this good pussy, you go outside and find some other skank?!"

The temperature dropped at least 10 degrees as I stood up, staring her dead in the face, noticing her poor makeup job trying to hide those crow's feet. She was much older than she was portraying.

The guys shifted nervously, their attention on us, except for his; he was blatantly staring at my ass. While I appreciated it, I felt he should have stepped in.

Nonetheless, orange crush barbie was about to lose her fucking teeth.

I sucked my teeth. "Honey, I'm nobody's skank, but keep talking and I'm about to make your dick sucking a lot easier."

With a pop of her gum, she gets dangerously close, her breath a whisper on my lips. "Yeah? Ask him where he was two days ago. Upstairs in his bed with his name all over my lips. I doubt he even washed sheets. I'm sure my orgasm is still all over them. You're a temporary fix. I'll have him back. They always come back."

Leaning back, she smirks, raising an eyebrow. I stood there and wondered why she didn't scream it to the heavens. They say silence tells it all. His was louder than a thunderstorm and he still says nothing, so maybe she's telling the truth... and it hurts.

I assumed he heard it, that they all had, but realized that maybe after years of riding that their hearing had dulled so her silent exchange was a means to lunge the blade, but not loud enough for him to react angrily towards her.

To think I satisfied myself to the thought of him in their dirty sheets disgusts me.

She smiled as if she won, and she had. That tidbit of info hurt me to the core. I did the only thing I could do and went upstairs. I started packing my bag, listening to those hyenas chuckle. I may not be safe at home, but it's the only place I have left to go to get away from him.

Cupid

As Lyric storms upstairs, I quickly snatch up Trix by the arm. She lets out a sexual moan, thinking I wanted her.

"What the fuck did you say to her?"

She pulled back angrily. "What does it matter? She's temporary, a play toy for you. I'm the one you want, baby."

If I wanted to claim you and your mediocre pussy, I would have. But almost everyone here has had you. Nobody's claiming you. You're a fuck and suck, and let's be honest, sweetie, Lolli is the master of sucking dick. So, why would I claim a useless, used-up disappointment?

"You're only lying to yourself! What can she do that I can't?"

"Easy, be a damn lady. Move..."

With a forceful push, I sent her tumbling onto the couch, where she landed awkwardly and almost fell off. I didn't care. I needed to sort this out.

I know I'm in for a firestorm and I'm prepared for it...I think. You know what, I better bring backup.

Lyric

I want to leave, leave this stupid place, and never return.
Why am I here, anyway?

All I want is to live on the beach and be happy. How the
fuck did I get to this situation I'm in now with a biker and a
screaming match with a hooker?

I look at myself in the mirror, willing the tears not to fall,
and then a flash of the horrible day hits me like a ton of
bricks, and I can't catch my breath. My breath hitches, a
frantic gasp escaping before I try to regain control, the
moment stretching before a panic attack fully takes hold.

Then I go back into his room and pack my stuff up. No
way in hell am I staying here. Maybe I'll get a room at the
hotel. I think I can afford three days max before I exhaust my
savings. No wait, I have an alternative. Just let me make sure
I have everything.

Cupid

Digi follows behind me. I opened the door, and she practically flew out, bag a mess, like she was late for something.

"Wait, where are you going?"

Her eyes bore into mine, a hardened gaze, before soft-
ening as she spotted Digi behind me, a clear wave of relief
washing over her.

"Digi, I was just about to come find you. Do you have
space in your room for one more?"

He looks at me, then at her. Uh, yeah I have bunk beds
you can take the top bunk, b-but d-don't you want to talk it
out?"

She smiled at him, then glared at me. "Not interested. Get back to your company, Cupid; she seems to miss you terribly. It's been three days. You must be desperate for some alone time together. Digi, where's your room?"

He speeds past, and she glares again before following.

That dirty, lying bitch!

I stomp back downstairs; Trix was now flirting with Club, but he wasn't the least bit interested after the spectacle.

Oh, but I'm the one you want, right? Fucking lying cum dumpster.

I walk up to Jackal. "Prez," I said, my voice tight with anger, "I demand an immediate ban on these girls; permanently prohibiting them from our clubhouse."

He knows I'm mad, completely pissed off. I want them out. They're nothing but trouble. They were crazy to think we cared at all about them. The only way they learn is to take the club away from them.

"You can't do that! Just because you want to screw some new random piece of ass, we got to leave?" She screeched as her girls backed her up.

"You lied. We never fucked three days ago, and I'll be damned if I let you harass her any further.

Jackal looks at everyone as Digi makes his way back. I need to make sure she knows that was a lie, but first, to ensure it doesn't happen again.

"That's a club vote. All those in favor of banishment say, aye."

"AYE!"

The vote was unanimous. Jackal chuckled, "Look, I never wanted you here. Get out, all of you, and don't come back.

Consider yourselves warned; Cheetah's orders are to shoot trespassers, and he's a damn good shot. Scram!" His voice boomed, and they scurried out of here. Good damn riddance!

Lyric

Disappointed by my response, I sat on the top bunk, feeling the heavy weight of regret settle upon me. I should have knocked her teeth down her cum laden throat. Her verbal assault was vicious. I haven't even known him long enough to get this mad. I need to sleep. Thank the heavens for bunk beds.

I took a super-hot shower, changed, and put my headphones on, figuring he'd come check on me.

Not tonight Cupid, keep your dirty arrow to yourself.

Cupid

After their eviction, Jackal looks at me. "You're not fooling anyone, Eros."

Calling me Cupid's Greek twin instead sometimes gives me a break from the Cupid crap.

"I know your story and your fears, but I bet it scares you more if she left or if Johnny got a hold of her, so fix this. Take it slow, but don't hold back. There's a reason you two crossed paths.

Ahhh... the wisdom of a love-stricken man. I hate to admit it, but he's right.

I trudge up the stairs. I know she can hear me. Digi's door creaks as it opens, and her back is towards me. I see a cord lying on her cheek. She put headphones in to tune me out.

What could I say, really? I didn't know what else Trixie said besides us fucking three days ago, but that was a lie to piss her off and run her away. I watched her for a few moments. Her hair was damp, and she put on a white tank top, but no bra straps. She wasn't wearing a bra.

"Did you fuck her three days ago?" Her voice startled me. I thought she was already asleep.

"Absolutely not."

"And I wasn't sleeping on cum stained sheets from your little romp with... flopsy?" You could practically hear the venom in her voice and a hint of humor.

She turned around; the blanket covering her chest as she looked at me.

I give a sly smile, "No darlin', I believe the only signs of an orgasm in my bed seem to be what you left behind earlier. Goodnight, kitten." I wink before walking out.

If she gasped any louder, she would have inhaled an earbud. Satisfied, I head to my room to wrap that sheet with her essence around my throbbing dick until I mixed with hers, fantasizing until it becomes real.

I'm in real trouble as Cupid tries to assassinate me with his arrow.

I hate that fat fucker...

Lyric

Gasp

I couldn't say anything. Instead of the burning shame, a strange, exhilarating freedom surged through me. Confirming he, indeed, knew about my personal playing session. I bet... he was going to jerk off. I'm confident the sound of me whispering his name as I shook to orgasm riled him up. I climbed down and tiptoed to his door. An eye for an eye, right? Besides, I can't deny I'm not curious about his "arrow".

Cupid

Moaning softly, I whisper, "Oh, baby... your touch feels so good." With closed eyes, I savor the sensation, feeling the wetness and slight throbbing while I stroke and twist. My heavy breathing fills the room, and arousal hangs in the air. A wave of warmth flooded me as I savored the imagined sweetness of her kisses, licking me up and down, then taking me down her throat. I fisted the sheet and brought it to my nose, inhaling her sweetness.

"Mmm Lyric..."

I picked up the pace and groaned until something brushed against me, and my eyes shot wide open.

There she was, my sexual obsession in the flesh, her soft, warm, supple flesh. She watches me until she peels her tank top off, revealing she was indeed wearing no bra and those tawny nipples were there in all their glory.

She moves the blanket aside, crawls in, and straddles me,

still in her delicate lace black thong, I felt the warmth radiating from her pussy.

My hands slide over, then grip her ass. I couldn't help but squeeze both her cheeks, which elicited a whispered moan from her.

She rocks against my dick while gazing at me. The temptation becomes too much to resist, and I place my thumb on her lip, feeling the sensation of her tongue grazing it before she sucks on it gently, causing an intense surge of sexual tension within me.

Her soft hand reached behind, stroking me, sending shivers of pleasure down my spine that made my eyes roll back. I regained my eyesight just in time to watch her lean forward, a hair away from my lips. She has lust radiating from her pores.

God, I want her.

I don't know if I should take her as I imagined or take it slowly, feeling her out, literally and figuratively.

She lightly presses her lips to mine; I feel her gasp as I pull her close by her neck and intensify the lip lock. She pulled back just enough to break the kiss, her sweet breath sweeping over mine.

"Please..." She whimpered as she rocked faster against me, wanting to get off so badly. I flip us, rip off her delicate underwear, to which she gasped and bit her lip.

I shook my head. "Slow down, darlin'. I've wanted nothing more than this moment. I am going to savor every inch of you."

The taste of her skin was intoxicating as I kissed her jawline, then her neck, finally settling on her collarbone. I murmured, "You're so sweet and sexy; I just want to hear you moan my name again, right this second." I kiss her jawline, neck, then her collarbone. "You're sweet and sexy and all I want is to hear you moan my name again." I trail her breasts, grazing her nipples.

"Oh, yes, just like that," she purred softly.

"You didn't realize it then, the way my eyes followed you at the bar, but you were mine from the start."

Her taste is pure bliss, sweet and irresistible, as I indulged in devouring and licking her until she came again and again. I watched her wriggle and writhe to my touch. "Oh Aleister, yes...it feels so good, baby."

I never want her to stop panting, moaning, or screaming my name. She pushes my head away from her throbbing clit and lets out a loud sigh as she moves us so she's on top again. I may be over six feet tall and 200+ pounds, but she is strong for her tiny stature.

She leans forward and kisses me gently. "That was better than I ever fantasized. Let me show you my gratitude."

Her full, crimson lips brush my cheek, then my chin, a feather-light touch before finding the soft skin of my neck. A sharp intake of breath as her teeth graze the barbells, a delicious, electric pain. Fuck!

I growl, watching her, as she finally reaches my swollen and neglected arrow. She blows on the tip and my entire body shudders as she giggles.

"Ooh, someone's eager, aren't they? Guess it has been more than three days." Chuckling at the lie that almost got me in trouble. I look down to her smirking, my dick resting on her lips. It jumps in anticipation. "Kitten, you have no idea."

She catches me off guard by deep throating my entire raging hard on. I couldn't hold back if I tried "Goddammit! Fuck, baby, just like that." She hums. The buzzing adds a whole new sensation that was fast tracking me to an explosive orgasm.

"Oh, baby. If you don't stop, I'm going to..." It was too late as she swallowed every drop of me and then smiled.

If this were a competition, then Lolli just dropped to second place.

I pulled her up to wrap my arms around her and kissed her forehead. As much as I wanted to seal the deal and screw her brains out, there was something stirring within me and that caused some anxiety. I called her mine so easily. Could I really tread down this path?

I didn't have the energy to conquer that hill of repressed emotion. I look down to see her swirling her fingers across my chest like last night. I brush my fingertips aimlessly across her back.

She hums for a bit, then stops. "You know, after the incident downstairs, I swore to myself that I wanted nothing to do with you." She sits up but doesn't cover up, and I'm pleasantly distracted.

She snaps her fingers. "Hey buddy, up here." She covers up so I can focus. What I wouldn't give for x-ray vision right now.

"Then when you told me you had... umm, heard me, I felt my entire body flush, and I knew you'd probably be in here jerking off. Using the spot where I came was an added bonus. I couldn't help but to peek and when I saw you moaning my name; I needed your touch because my body was on fire."

I reach down to squeeze her ass, causing her to slide her leg up to rest on my upper thigh. I looked down and got lost in her gorgeous eyes.

Talking about our solo sessions reminded me to ask her

what I was curious about. " Speaking of self pleasure, I have to be honest with you about something, listening to you on the other side of the door, well that's not exactly the first time I heard you by yourself."

She looked genuinely shocked. "What? I've only done it once since I've been here."

"Well, you see, last night after you regained consciousness and hopped in my arms you fell asleep, but you, uh, put your hand between your legs, then slipped them in your pants..."

I stopped, letting her piece together the puzzle. Her expression said it all, pure horror and utter embarrassment. She didn't even realize she had done it.

"So, you're saying... I?"

"All over these pretty little fingers before you went back to sleep." I kiss her fingertips, the same ones. "Do you always do that in your sleep?"

I think my question horrified her even more.

"I-I don't know! It's been a few months since my ex stranded me here. Maybe it was stress related?"

She tried to find a suitable excuse. I couldn't resist. "Does that include moaning my name at climax?"

Her hand flew to her mouth. "Oh my god, I didn't. Did I? Oh god..."

She buries her face into my armpit, thankful I don't smell like a biker. We have that reputation of smelling like the open road. I smell like my favorite cologne that was a rich blend of aged tobacco leaf and creamy vanilla with secondary combinations of spices, tonka bean and cacao. It was a scent that was simple yet unforgettable.

"As if I hadn't already embarrassed myself earlier, you pile that on?!" I pull her tighter against me and lift her chin, so it meets close enough that I lean down and kiss her. She seemed to relax and gave me a half smile.

"You taste delicious just wait until I have all of you."

She squeaks as I poke her side. She settles down, and it's a comfortable silence until we both fall asleep.

Lyric

The next morning, I wake up and turn over to face a grinning idiot.

"Mornin' sunshine."

I growl, "Let's be clear. I am not a morning person. If you are, then leave me be, you fucking psychopath."

I turn away, my entire back exposed, and he places kisses, causing me to moan, then he stops at my shoulder, biting gingerly.

"No problem, I'll hop in the shower and leave you be." He smacks my ass before getting up. I can't help but take a glance at his deliciously tattooed back. While he was at his dresser fishing out clothes, I asked him about his tattoos since they were so massive on his muscular frame. He laughs as he explains them. He has a skull being the main focal point surrounded by various biker related pieces to include a sick Harley Davidson bike, a bar girl pouring a glass of scotch and the club emblem across his shoulders, *Fratres usque ad mortem,* he says it meant Brothers till Death. I nod as he goes into the bathroom and I doze into a peaceful slumber, dreaming of a certain handsome devil.

Cupid

The scalding water, a soothing weight against my aching back. A low hum vibrates from the jets. What have I gotten myself into? Her beauty is breathtaking, a vision of sunlight and grace. Why would an angel even glance my way, let alone want anything to do with a flawed creature like me? The warm water feels heavy, almost suffocating.

All the doubt and fear came rushing forward as I watched her sleep.

Lyric

I've been hanging out with the guys for five days now and it's been an emotional roller coaster with him. He gets close and pulls away and it's so random I don't know which one I encounter first.

After bunny-gate, as the guys call it, we had an intense yet passionate night, even though we didn't have sex. But the next morning, he was out the door and on his bike before I came downstairs. I was hoping to hang out. He came back that night after dinner around 10 pm and didn't even acknowledge my presence, just went into the kitchen. I felt uncomfortable, so I said goodnight and went to sleep in Digi's room.

The next morning, I awoke to the warmth of his body next to mine; the scent of his cologne and the feel of his arm around me. I don't know if I walked in or if he picked me up, but here I was. I was still wearing my sleep clothes, so nothing had happened. Maybe he missed me because I missed his touch. But I still felt miffed.

This went on for days—the disappearances, shrouded in secrecy, with the flimsy excuse of it being "club business", but nobody else went with him. How much business can they have in this small ass town?

I felt like he was pushing me away; I mean, he hated love. What chance did I have? I wanted to be the person to break the curse, to show him it's not all bad. I couldn't deny it. I liked him, and I wanted him to like me, too.

Anyway, the afternoon sun warmed my face and the faint smell of fresh cut grass surrounded me as I sat on the swing in the backyard, lost in thought; he'd ridden off again, somewhere unknown.

Where?

Who the hell knows? I was frustrated!

I shouldn't be. I hardly know him or his backstory, but I wanted to, and he just wasn't letting me in. We still haven't had sex yet, and I was questioning if he wanted me at all. I exhale forcefully as I drop my head into my hands.

"Hey, try not to overthink his behavior; it'll only stress you out. I know exactly what he's doing. He's a man of terrible habit."

I looked over to see Jackal taking up the rest of the space on the swing. He uses his strong legs to push us further than I had, and I sat back to enjoy the breeze.

"Is it me?" I reluctantly ask as my voice cracks.

"Not at all. Aleister has been through a tough situation that makes him clam up at the thought of approaching love or feeling it. It's a wall he put up after his mother died and nobody's been special enough to tear it down. Not until you. He's fighting with himself and the years of being a cold, heartless bastard. You need to know the complete story and maybe you can help him understand that it's okay to feel."

He stares out at the mountains and sighs; I take his hand because Digi told me about his great love and losing her to cancer. She sounded like an angel. He looks over as I smile.

"You're a good man for these boys and I'm sure she's watching down on you, smiling at how good you've taken care of them. Just...don't forget about yourself."

He smiles, taking in a big breath of air before exhaling. Cheetah sticks his head out from the kitchen door, "Hey Lyric, there's a man here to see you."

Me? Who even knows I'm here? I walk through the house to see a tall man with blonde hair and grey eyes sitting on the couch in a cheap suit. He stands when he notices my presence.

"Miss Pullman?"

"Yes?"

He holds out his hand for me to shake. "I'm Dillon McDermott from Trisler & Scott law firm. I have been assigned to Mr. Adams' estate."

"You mean Dave."

"Yes, can we discuss his final arrangements?" I motion for him to sit back on the sofa and I sit beside him. I was curious because I thought this was done with immediate family. I was just his employee.

"Mr. Adams' will and testament was very simple and pretty straightforward since he had no family or children..."
"Mr. Adams' will and testament was very simple and pretty straightforward since he had no family or children..." A

heavy, rhythmic thudding announced someone in thick-soled boots; then, silence.

We both looked up, and Aleister was glaring at us, Dillon mostly, and he was pissed. Typical biker possessiveness, don't know how that works when he hasn't even staked claim, so I ignore him and continue my talk with Dillon, not even bothering to introduce him. He walks off somewhere.

"Go on, Dillon."

He shuffles some papers and nervously clears his throat. How cute.

"Well, to be blunt, Miss Pullman, Dave left the bar and all his assets to you."

"WHAT?!" I shot up. I didn't mean to yell and grab the attention of everyone, but I did not see that coming. That sweet man, my rescuer in my darkest hour, gave me all his earthly possessions, and now I was responsible. I felt the tears form.

Oh, Dave.

Cupid was the first to come in. I knew he hadn't gone far after seeing us. I'm sure he was listening close by somewhere.

"Hey, what's wrong?" He slides his arm around my waist and pulls me to him.

I see what you're doing there.

I quickly step out of his grasp and wrap my arms around myself. "Dillon told me that Dave left everything to me, including the bar. I own Cinnamon Alley."

I'm ignoring that he's trying to stare Dillon down and intimidate him, which he was. Dillon was moving uncomfortably in his gaze. He tried to remain professional, despite the fact.

"Yes, and his insurance will cover the expenses of any

remodeling or renovation you may need to re-open. Here is their contact information for questions you may have and mine if you need assistance. The assets, if liquidated, total $350,000, not including the bar."

My legs gave out, and I sat down in shock. He left me so much money. I could finally leave! Then realization hit, or rather, my heart sank.

I look at Aleister, then Dillon, getting up to shake Dillon's hand. "Thank you, Dillon. We'll talk again. I need time to digest everything."

"No problem, Lyric. Call anytime if you need anything." I glanced at Cupid. He wasn't pleased I got a guy's number right in front of him, but that's his problem, not mine.

"Thank you. I will speak to you soon." He nods and then looks between us before leaving quickly.

I run my hands through my hair as I pace the living room with my thoughts. Dave left me the bar and $350 grand. I could leave tomorrow for the beach and buy a nice home, but then again, I couldn't shut down the bar, it's the only bar in town. It was my saving grace.

"That's a stroke of luck, isn't it? What are you going to do, Lyric?" I look at Digi, whose childlike face was just so positive and innocent.

I shrug my shoulders. "I don't know. I have enough money to leave this place and finally find my dream home on the beach, but..." I glanced over, "I loved that bar, and Dave loved me enough to trust me with his estate. I... I just don't know."

"You can't open that bar. It's too dangerous and I won't let you..." He states so matter-of-factly.

Spinning towards the sound of his voice, eyebrow raised.

"YOU don't have a say in this. What's it to you, anyway?" I spat, the words tasting bitter on my tongue.

You could hear a pin drop and feel how extremely awkward everyone felt. I didn't mean to bring it up in front of everyone, but I did. He doesn't say a word.

"Whatever." I huffed.

I was too angry to stick around, so I stormed out and headed to the bar. It wasn't far, or maybe the distance itself was what I needed. But I also needed to assess the damage to see if it was even worth saving. If not, I could leave this awful place and him behind.

Cupid

She walked away from me. I couldn't bring myself to tell her not to go. The words caught in my throat, a heavy silence hanging in the air as my heart remained stubbornly closed.

Do you ever wish you could change a single moment, avoiding a past loss and finally understanding the depth of love and joy?

Well, I didn't get to relive that moment and my mom never recovered from the pain of heartbreak instead she found another way to hurt.

After Mr. Wellington and having her committed, mother seemed to bounce back to some form of her former self, but not quite. She went from the 60s contoured sheath style dress to wearing tight leather capri pants and tight skirts, hanging out at Cinnamon Alley with the socially depraved. She became a social drinker and came in all hours of the night. And sometimes she was not alone.

One night I went to check on her and there was my mother straddling the lap of Johnny Picardio and they were making out heavily.

"Ugh, hello, mother. Could you dial it back while your son is in the house?" She hops off his lap, and he smirks at me. I knew instantly that I didn't like him, sitting there all cocky and arrogant. He didn't move other than to wipe her signature lipstick off his lips.

"Oh, hey. This is my friend Johnny, Johnny, my son."

"I know who he is." The sharpness in his voice instantly put me on edge. My mother, though grown, was utterly help-less around men, and that made me fiercely protective.

She stands in front of me, eyeing my clenched fists. "Hey, what are you doing here?"

"Do I need a reason? I was making sure you're okay."

"I'm fine, see? You can go now." She pushed me toward the door.

I could see she was hopeless. "Oh, no need to kick me out because of your pathetic little boy toy. I'll gladly leave, but don't call me when he hurts you." I snatch my hand from hers and storm out.

She was love struck again.

And I would not stand around and watch.

Lyric

The damage, while significant, is repairable; a thorough cleaning and rearrangement, it could be the main attraction once more. You can almost smell the fresh paint and feel the renewed energy.

"I didn't ask for a babysitter, you know." I look over to see Blondie leaning against the door frame and smoking a cigarette.

"Not leaving you alone in this place. I promised I'd protect you. Now, I know you're upset at Cupid..."

"Upset? I'm fucking livid! Don't know why I should even care. We haven't even had sex yet."

Okay, that WAS NOT supposed to come out.

And his raised eyebrow said it all. "Sorry, I shouldn't have said that out loud." He just nods, exhaling the menthol smoke of his cigarette as I jot down a few notes.

I look back at him, "So what's your deal, anyway? You could be a world-famous model with your one-of-a-kind good looks, yet here you are. What gives?"

He flicks the cigarette away and steps inside the saloon doors. "The very qualities you find beautiful were once the target of relentless bullying throughout my life; it's a bitter truth. I drifted from Cali to Vegas, then Tucson, and one day I ended up here and nobody ragged on me. Many were curious, thought I was albino. Reckon I should stay, but I didn't have any money. So, I slept against the side of this bar when Jackal found me and offered me a place to stay. Been like a father figure ever since. That's my deal. What about you?"

My shoes step on broken glass and I take note. "Pretty simple, I had an asshole of a druggie boyfriend who stranded me here with nothing but my clothes and a phone. Dave took a chance on me, gave me a job, money to get my place, and I couldn't be more grateful that he did." I sniffle back the tears as I think about the crime scene and the cruel way his life ended.

"What about your parents?" He sticks close as I continue to survey.

I laugh out loud. "I don't have parents. Parents show emotion, like love and adoration. What I had were humans who couldn't even do that right. Me and my brothers fended for ourselves. I was their mother! While mommy was too busy climbing, and sleeping, up the corporate ladder, stay-at-home daddy was too busy drinking his sorrows away, reflecting on his failures, including a failed marriage, and took his misfortunes out on us. He was jealous of mom's success. He knew she was screwing around, but we were the closest thing he could hit." I shrug my shoulders as I turn off the lights and walk past him.

"Wow, that's deep."

"Yeah. Fucked up family to fucked up boyfriend, ready to go?" He simply nods.

On our way back, a familiar shadow appears near the clubhouse entrance.

"Oh great, just when I had forgotten my troubles at home."

Blondie chuckles. "The kid's crazy about you. Don't know how to express it." I don't even know what to say. Blondie squeezes me into a half hug before heading towards the garage.

I avoid the direct route as I wander side to side to give myself more time to think of what to say.

I think he knows what I'm doing, so he beelines straight towards me, pulls me in and kisses me hard and deep. It feels like heaven and when I pull back, he's gazing at me.

He's so mouth-wateringly gorgeous.

"Sell the place."

Until he opened his stupid mouth. What the fuck, man?

My anger flared, a hot, burning sensation forcing me to take a step back.

"Fucking Christ, way to ruin a perfect moment! I thought we were making up, but you just want to control me. You're impossible! And let me be clear: I'm NOT selling, and I WILL run the place after renovations. Do you understand? This is not up for discussion!"

It's a knock down drag out fight in the front yard. I see a few blinds ruffle from different parts of the house.

"No, I don't hear you, Lyric, because it's stupid and you're going to get yourself killed. You think Johnny's just forgotten about what you did to him? He's going to hurt you; he's going to hurt *me* by hurting you. I can't let that happen again."

"What do you mean again?" I saw a break in his tough guy persona before it came roaring back.

"Doesn't matter, I won't allow it and that's final."

The laughter bubbled up, uncontrollable—not a sweet giggle, but a harsh, incredulous sound, bordering on manic, a raw, ragged burst of disbelief that clawed its way out.

"That's cute, real cute. Listen here, I am going to renovate, clean up, and open that bar. Dave trusted ME with his bar and his money. What I'd rather do is leave this godforsaken town in the dust and never look back to find my little love nest on the beach, but I won't. And do you know why? It's you, you overprotective neanderthal nitwit! I want to be with you! I want to be with you, but you won't fully commit, and I'm exhausted. Tired of fighting, tired of waiting. So, if you won't even try, I'm burying myself in work and planning my escape...including leaving this town."

I fought back the tears, the lump in my throat tightening, but the emotion was too strong, and my eyes quickly filled. I tried to step past him, but he grabbed my arm and spun me around.

"Don't! Touch me."

"Is that what you really want? To leave this place?"

"No! I want YOU, but it's obvious I don't have a chance. Maybe you should get those slut bunnies back. I'm sure you'd like someone who can service you without commitment."

I snatch away and storm into the house, telling Digi I'd be in his room again.

I hate feeling like this.

Cupid

DAMMIT! I can't seem to say the right thing or anything at all. I know Jackal said to be honest and forthcoming, but that's easier said than done. My memories are no fairytale and proof positive that love doesn't exist.

I stormed into the house, headed to the bar, grabbed a bottle of scotch, and made myself scarce. She didn't need someone like me, but that doesn't mean I wouldn't watch after her since she insists on opening that bar.

Lyric

It's been a rough but productive two weeks; I barely spend my free time at the house anymore. I hired contractors to do the reconstruction and remodel, while I took the wheel in decorating Cinnamon Alley but didn't take away from the rough cowboy saloon theme. I only enhanced it, adding two new 90" rustic, modern pool tables, new swivel upholstered bar stools and sturdier tables. Dave was right, there would always be a fight, so I purchased several handguns and a bat propped up next to Dave's shotgun.

My current deep cleaning of the bar went awry because of my outfit choice: a white tank top, distressed jean shorts, and cowboy boots. I wasn't expecting to clean. I wanted to see if I needed any more bar glasses before I made a bulk order. But with my frustration, one thing led to another and now I'm practically running a wet t-shirt contest after I washed and waxed the bar surface. I didn't even hear the doors swing open.

"Excuse me, Miss, are you open?"

I looked up to see a man in a dark gray three-piece suit,

his polished shoes gleaming oddly amidst the dirt; he was definitely out of place.

"Um, no, not yet, sir. We will open in a few days. Sorry."

He checks his gold watch, a glint of light flashing off the surface, and gives me a devilish smile. "It's okay. Sad I won't be here when you open, but maybe next time I conduct business in town. I'll get to see the place in all its glory and perhaps buy the pretty lady a drink?"

I watch as his eyes travel down to my soaked shirt and cherry red bra underneath. I cleared my throat; he was pretty handsome for a much older gentleman. He was tall with dark brown hair and an intense stare. He had familiar eyes, even though I'm certain I've never seen him before. The expensive tailored suit just wrapped him up in a pretty package.

"Have a nice day, miss." He walked out. He was definitely out of his element. Wonder what he was doing here? It didn't matter. I finished up cleaning and by 8 pm Digi was waiting to walk me home.

We walked at a relaxed pace; him kicking rocks in the road with his hands in his pockets. "Are y-you and C-Cup-Cupid broken up now?" He is so adorable with his bashfulness around the fairer sex.

"We were never together, dear. He made sure of that."

"Is that w-why you're staying in my room?"

"Sort of. I really am sorry for crowding your space. I can sleep on the couch if it's too much."

"No! I l-like having you there. You're like the big sister I never had and... you help me understand stuff about girls. I still don't think I could talk to a girl, but I'm getting more comfortable talking to you, so that's a win." He shrugs and I laugh. His innocence is pure and after hearing about how he was dumped by his group of so-called friends, we share a weird bond of being abandoned here.

The aroma of roast chicken and potatoes filled the air as we entered, and I was starving. All eyes, wide and curious, fell on me; I'd completely forgotten my soaked t-shirt, the damp fabric clinging and revealing far too much. A blush heated my cheeks as their gazes quickly darted away, except for his. His dark, intense eyes locked on mine, and he couldn't look away.

"I have to change; I'll be right back." I tell Digi, and he says he'll fix me a plate. I take a mind-numbingly hot shower. Then, find my grey leggings and burgundy crop sweatshirt that shows the bottom of my lacy blue bra if I lift my arms too far up. I wanted to tease, make him drool or suffer, whatever got it through his thick head.

I bounce down the stairs. The crop top bounces up and down with me. I skip into the kitchen to see Digi and Cupid eating at the table and talking. Then they stop.

Want to guess what they might be talking about? Yeah, me, either.

"Hey Digi, where's my plate?"

"Microwave, Cupid warmed it up for you." I saw a hint of a smile.

Great.

"Uh, thanks." I grab my plate and a fork. "Hey, I'll be trying to master level 12 of Brick Invaders. Whenever you're done, you can show me how to get unlimited lives. Night!" I chose to avoid him. All he was going to do was stare with those intense eyes, trying to get me to change my mind. It's not my mind that needs changing.

Cupid

"Well, did she say anything?" I knew she was close to Digi, like brother and sister, especially since she's been bunking in his room since the blowout.

He just shrugs his shoulders. He doesn't want to side with anyone; he wants us to reconcile, but doesn't want to get in the middle.

Besides, he's just a kid.

I sighed, doomed to resign to another night without sleep. It has been horrible, basically nonexistent without her. She's changed my dynamic so much. Knowing she's close and I can't touch her drives me crazy.

I understand her needs, but I'm still fighting my own demons, but I had to find a way to make her understand. It was true. I wanted her.

Lyric

Opening night! Cinnamon Alley's grand reopening attracted a decent crowd. Most of the guys came to celebrate and, naturally, keep an eye on me. They've grown to be my big brothers and I am so glad to feel safe.

He's not here, though.

Cheetah said he went for a ride, but that was hours ago. He's been doing that a lot. I busy myself, tending the bar and tables, since I'm the only one working.

Digi volunteers to wash the dishes and clear the tables. Cheetah is operating as security/bouncer. Knox is playing darts with some pretty blonde and Blondie is dancing with a brunette and they're getting mighty cozy.

Jackal saddles up to the bar and smiles. "You really love this place, don't you?" I slide him over a chilled glass of Redemption, a nine-year-old bourbon. I look around at the people enjoying their time here and smile, "It's what I always wanted it to be, no low lives, just townsfolk enjoying being out of the house."

He tips his glass, sets down a bill and walks over to Knox and challenges him to a game of darts. It looks like they're betting a substantial amount of money.

Glancing from the corner of my eye, I noticed someone on a bar stool and turned to look. A hot, prickly anger flares within me as her smug grin widens, and then, with a sharp snap of her fingers, it ignites.

Lord, save me from snatching her up.

I take a deep breath..

"So, *you* own the bar now, sad shame. It's probably your fault Dave is dead. At least, that's what I heard."

That's probably the lie you've been spreading, you vindictive, cum guzzling whore.

"Did you come in to cause trouble because I have a business to run? I know you have an hourly rate I can afford, but I'm just so busy."

Trixie glared at me. "Have you seen MY baby, Cupid? I know he's missing my pussy so much. I'm sure you don't even compare to the tricks I can pull. Plus, I miss playing with his long, thick, straight... arrow." She licks her lips as she fantasizes.

She was trying to provoke me. "If you're looking for him, why is your cheap ass here?"

She sneered at my comment, but quickly recovered. "Well, he's been following you around like a lost little puppy. I thought I'd find him up mommy's skirt." I feel my jaw clench at her condescending tone. "Well, he isn't. You and your dick sucking lips can probably find him at the house, so you can go now."

"Aww... gladly. Hope we aren't too loud when your return, but I can't help myself he just feels so fucking amazing." Her tone and smile are nauseating as she hops off the stool.

I got to remember to sanitize where she sat, don't want someone catching syphilis.

She pulled down her cheap leather skirt and left quickly. Guess I better not go home anytime soon I may toss my dinner hearing them mid-fuck. I sigh as I wipe the counter with frustrated aggression. I hate that cum slurping gutter bitch! What I wouldn't give to shut her up, but she won again. She got him, and I was heartbroken.

Whatever, I'm over it.

I tell myself that, but my heart says differently.

Cupid

The silence was heavy, broken only by the occasional rustle of leaves, an absence of the usual nature sounds, like birds or crickets.

I've been spending a lot of time up here...with her. "I miss you so much. The only person who has had my heart was you and now... I'm so... I don't know."

I take a swig of Balvenie 12-year-old scotch as I place the dozen white roses in front of her and sigh. Sometimes I just need to meet with her and get the thoughts out, the ones that scare me, the ones that plague me at night, the thoughts about Lyric.

The moonlight shadows my bike and the small lake across from where she's buried. I chose this spot because she loved the water. It was her healing mechanism. She always came back and was ready to grab hold of life and seek her own personal happiness, but a man always came, skewed her plan, and sent her barreling off course.

There's a lot of my mother in Lyric, perhaps that's why I run. I don't want to be the cause of her regret. She said it herself. She wanted to leave this hellhole, but she wanted to stay... because of me.

And what have I got to offer?

I can't even warm my frigid heart to the thought of building something with her. I pushed her away and I'll have to live with that.

God, I'm an idiot.

I kiss the headstone, "I love you, mom. I miss you."

I head back into town, wondering if I should stop by the bar. It's still early, so I do. I park next to my brother's bikes. I'm glad they stepped up to watch after her. The music grows louder as I approach. It aligned with the country theme of the bar. Instead of walking in, I leaned forward. There she was, in the middle of the dance floor, but not alone. She was being spun and twirled by that lawyer jerk. He smiled widely as he watched her enjoy his hands all over her. Her smile seemed so bright. I stepped back and headed home.

Who was I to get in the way?

Lyric

Did he really think I wouldn't see him at the door? The one person I was hoping to celebrate with? He thought I wouldn't notice him. He's freaking massive! My heart had been waiting all night, hoping. He did, but left, and I know why.

Dillon had come by to congratulate me on the opening and asked for a dance. I thought no harm of it, but I was wrong because he spotted us and then left. That'll probably drive him right back to Trixie.

After said dance, Dillon asked me out on a friendly date.

I politely turned him down. He's not Cupid but no point in waiting, right? Still, my heart wasn't in it.

Soon, the bar was closing on my first successful day and without a fight, I might add. I still dreaded going home. My heart couldn't bear to hear him with her, but I sucked it up because I was riding with the guys. Even though a short distance they wouldn't take no for an answer.

We get home and the lights are off.

Please don't let her be there.

Some guys push their bikes to the garage while I try to dismount Blondie's gracefully.

I stand at the beginning of the pathway to the door. I am hesitating to go in. I take smaller steps to prolong the inevitable. I actively pray not to hear her wailing and moaning or the squeak of bedsprings.

Digi runs back from going inside. It was as if he was checking to see if they were there so he could warn me. He whispers something to Club who was at the door. Club nods his head, then gestures for me to come. "Don't worry Lyric, he's out back on the swing, alone and drinking."

I felt a huge relief as I picked up my pace. Just as I was about to pass Club, he stopped me.

"There's something you should know. Something really important he doesn't talk about. He'll kill me, but it explains a lot. Today is the anniversary of his mother's death. He takes it real hard. I know you two are squabbling, but take it easy on him."

I didn't know. I would have postponed the bar opening if I'd known.

I meander to the backyard door and let it creak loudly. So he knows someone's approaching. I see him rocking the swing a bit, but no other movement. I catch the swing going forward and sit down, then our eyes meet.

A soft whisper escaped my lips; barely audible. "I'm sorry about your mother. Why didn't you tell me? I would have opened another day. I would have been here for you."

He's still staring straight ahead into the darkness. "You remind me so much of her when she was my stable, loving mom and not chasing after some...man. Beautiful, independent, so much life, but then, one after another, they snuffed her out."

He takes a huge chug from the bottle that he held on the other side. "Stop." I plead. Taking the bottle and place it on the ground near me.

He sighs, leaning forward while rubbing his hands together. "I should have gone up and checked on her immediately after she stormed upstairs, but I was so used to her moping. I didn't know this was the breaking point. I could have saved her and she'd still be alive."

I take his hand, the calluses rough against my softer skin. I place our joined hands on my thigh, giving it a reassuring pat. I look at him until his eyes find mine.

"Tell me, tell me what happened."

Cupid

I wanted to clam up and run away. My guys only know bits and pieces of the story. They are aware of her anniversary because I visit her grave.

"Aleister, If you want me to understand, tell me. We can stay out here all night. I'm not going anywhere."

She scoots over and leans against me, laying her head on my arm because she couldn't quite reach my shoulder because of our height difference. She rubs circles between my thumb and forefinger. I close my eyes and inhale deeply; she smells like lilac and roses this time.

I rock the swing back and forth, enjoying the slight breeze we get. My hands, initially clasped tightly in her comforting grip, loosen slightly, the tension leaving my fingertips as I try to share my story.

Before I could utter a word, a deafening crash, followed by blood-curdling screams, erupted from the house.

I never jumped up so fast, and she was right behind me. I push her behind me, "If I say run, you run, you hear me?" She nods and then jumps again when we hear another scream.

The house was pitch black until Cheetah flicked a light on, his finger on the trigger. Thank god he wasn't a 'shoot-first-ask-questions-later' person.

Digi lay groaning on the ground, a head wound that was beginning to bleed, surrounded by shattered lamp fragments. Trixie appeared disheveled with her top torn, makeup smeared, and a frantic look on her face. She rushed towards me the moment she saw me.

"Oh Cupid, he tried to assault me! I was looking for you and he wouldn't take no for an answer! His hands were all over me, trying to rip my clothes off! See? I was so scared! Where were you? I needed you, baby!"

Lyric

Cautiously following, I find him in the living room, feminine looking hands barely encircling his waist. I know those tacky, cheap press-on nails anywhere! I'm distracted by Knox and Club helping Digi to his feet. He was bleeding from the head. After tending to many of my sibling's wounds from good old Daddy Dearest, I've learned to treat multiple contusions, bruises, deep cuts, and black eyes. I was practically an in-house nurse.

But Digi's wound looked gruesome. "Oh my God, Digi! What happened? Where's your first aid kit? Get it now!" I didn't have time to get it myself because the cut was deep. I needed to keep pressure on it. I don't think it's deep enough for him to go to the hospital, but we have to stop the bleeding. He risks infection if not treated and bandaged promptly though.

While I wait, I turn and see Trixie clinging to him and crying. He stands there stiffly. I know exactly what she's doing. Playing the cheap whore in distress. Sorry, damsel in distress card.

"Oh, Cupid, I was so afraid! I didn't want it! What if he had hurt me or forced himself on me? He's a monster!" She cries into Aleister's chest.

He unexpectedly shoved her to the ground, catching her off guard.

"Get off me. We all know you're lying! Everyone just got back not too long ago, including Digi. I was in the backyard for the last hour and a half. Of all people you pick to corner, and accuse in your little lie, you pick the most innocent one. The only one of us, besides Prez, who hasn't had a sample of your worn out snatch. Jeez, you're fucking pathetic! Why are you even here? We barred you."

She tries to reach for him, but he holds up his hand and takes a step back.

She looks horrified that he isn't comforting her. "What do you mean? I came to see you, baby. I missed you and I know you missed me, too."

Ugh, I wanted to puke, but I remained focused on Digi's wound. I pour peroxide on a few cotton balls to clean the wound, causing him to hiss. Once clean, I rub an ointment and bandage his wound. He's still kind of out of it, and I know he is in for one hell of a headache.

I guess that's when she finally noticed *my* presence after being so enamored by him.

"What the fuck is she doing here?" Trix points to me. "Tell her to leave! Now!"

Ooh... someone's upset.

I couldn't help but chuckle to myself. I walk towards her with purpose on ruining her fucking life. "Not that it's any of your business, but I live here with them and I'm not going anywhere, sweetheart."

She looks flabbergasted as I continue. "Ohhh, I see. You

thought because I wasn't running after Aleister that you could suck and fuck your way back in? You assaulted this poor boy and claimed he tried to attack you? He would never deal with the likes of someone like *you*. I barely understand why anyone would, but hey, no judgement about someone who gives it away for free. If I was a dude and it was the easiest way to get a nut..." I rattled off, letting the silence speak volumes. Letting my insults sink in. I know she needed a minute.

I saw the moment it all registered. She storms up to me. "You're lying. No girl has ever lived here, except that dumpy little..."

Before she could finish, I smacked the shit out of her and dared her to make one move. "You disrespectful cunt! Don't you dare talk ill about Miss Paige like that? Know your fucking place or lose your goddamned teeth. A real woman would never!"

The guys were frozen, watching us.

She's still clutching her face, but I can see my handprint. "You bitch!" She screams but still doesn't move. I stay ready just in case, obviously, she doesn't fight fair.

"Oh, you haven't seen the bitch in me yet, but you're about to!"

She spins around to him, producing pathetic pity tears. "She's lying, isn't she, baby?! And how come she gets to call you by your name? You bastard! You said we had to call you by your club name only!"

You could see his obvious irritation.

"Because you're nothing but used goods. I don't know how to get it through your thick head that we are nothing, never have been, and never will be. Yes, she lives here, and she stays with me because *she's* special to *me*."

Whoa! Didn't see that coming. They say the first step is admittance.

She locks eyes with me and then at him.

Have you ever seen a skank just lose it? You're about to...

"You bastard! You never loved anyone! You're a cold-hearted, stubborn asshole, but she waltzes in and suddenly you're in love?! That's absolute bullshit, you're not capable of loving someone all because of your screwed-up mother! You're a weak, pathetic mama's boy with a fear of commitment!"

His fists go stark white with how tightly he had them clutched. I step between them to keep him from doing something stupid.

"You better leave now, or I'll break that pretty little face of yours, you got that?" I said firmly.

She stared me down.

I was so focused on her, I nearly jumped when I felt his arm wrap around me and pull me towards his chest, my ass pressed against his...*oh my...*

Just concentrate on being angry, Lyric, not the pulsing stiffness pressing into your backside. I want nothing more than to feel it as he rams into me deeply, over and over and... oh god!

Trixie eyes his arm around me, then us together, as I try my best not to topple over the orgasmic wave I'm riding. I squeeze my legs tighter, but that makes the pulsing stronger.

She looks around at everyone watching our interaction and hisses.

"This isn't over... not by a long shot. I'll have the last laugh, I promise you. Count your days, bitch."

"Whatever you say... just leave, NOW!" I yelled back.

You're fucking with my orgasm, you raggedy bitch.

She continues to glare at me while walking out.

There was a collective exhale. Everyone looks at me wide-eyed in shock.

"Goddamn! This kitten's got claws! Nice..." Cheetah slaps me five and chuckles. I give myself slowly from Aleister's grasp to continue Digi a once-over. It doesn't stop the throbbing sensation between my legs from my almost orgasm.

"Hey sunshine, how are you feeling?"

He winces, but tries to produce a smile to stop my worrying. "Go on up, take some extra strength aspirin, and get some rest but sit propped up and the guys will check on you periodically, okay?" He nods as Jackal takes his arm, "Come on kiddo, you'll stay in my room where I can keep an eye on you."

Club dad reporting for duty.

They help him to his feet and up the stairs. I sigh, running my fingers through my hair as I look around at the destruction on the floor. I can't deal with this after everything. I'll deal with it in the morning.

I exhaled hard. "What a wild night." I say to no one in particular.

I turn around and he's right behind me. He's six feet of delicious, tattooed muscle, and his gaze is on me. His eyes, dark and smoldering, said it all. The warm, musky scent of his skin and cologne, a tantalizing blend, hung in the air, making my mouth water.

I barely had time to breathe before his mouth was on mine, a ravenous, consuming kiss that left me breathless.

I should be furious, but this electric thrill is coursing through me, silencing my anger. He pulls me upstairs and into his room. Not that I could fight him. After hoisting me over his shoulder, he jokingly swatted my ass, then lovingly stroked and kneaded it. The door slammed with a resounding ***thwack***, with the hard wood pressed against my back. His hands, rough yet firm, pinned my arms above my head. The rasp of his breath on my neck was hot, a prelude to the sharp bite that drew a moan from my lips.

That's going to leave a hickey.

He lets go of my hands to peel off everything I have on. In no time, I stand there completely naked, and he lets out a growl. "Oh, baby... fuck. Don't move, stay right there."

He walks into the bathroom and I hear the shower start and he comes out shirtless. His body is perfect and I just want to lick every inch.

You know what, I AM going to lick every inch...

He pulls me close, his arms a warm, enveloping cage, lifting me effortlessly. The bathroom's humid air, thick with the scent of his soap, hangs heavy as he carries me into the steaming shower. Warm water, a soothing cascade, drums a rhythmic beat against my back.

My legs wrap around his waist and he presses me up against the wall, the water cascading over him now as he nibbles and kisses his way from my lips down to my collarbone. Now with his beard and hair wet, he looked even more mouthwatering. He leans down and attacks my perky sensitive nipples; he knows how that riles me.

A breathless, "Right there..." escaped my lips.

I want him. I want this man like no other. My pussy is throbbing, screaming to be penetrated by the thickness that now stood proudly between my legs. I slide one arm down to stroke him, feeling his appreciative moans vibrating against my breasts. My nails draw a burning trail across his back as I kiss his neck and shoulders, his ragged groans fueling my desire, pushing me to leave my mark. I lap the water pouring off his chest like a thirsty sex kitten.

I can't take it anymore. "Baby, please."

"What? What do you want me to do?"

"Fuck me."

He leans back and we stare at each other as the water pours over the heated exchange between us. "There's nothing I've wanted more."

The feeling I felt as he slid me down onto him. I felt like a virgin losing it for the first time, but I was no virgin. Who the hell was I fucking before? Because this... this was magical. My body shook and quivered as he slammed into me. His grunts and groans were music to my ears.

"Oh, baby...baby. You're so tight, you feel so damn good. Oh..."

He buries himself deeper into me, and I can't contain my cries of pleasure anymore. I know they can probably hear me, but I'm in too much ecstasy to care. I feel my orgasm nearing and I see the signs he's close, too. For good measure, and to live out my previous fantasy, I pinch his nipples and twist the barbells.

He growls and speeds up his intensity, "Fuck baby, keep doing that." He buries his head in my neck as he grinds harder, slamming me down against him.

"Right there...there...don't stop!" He's hitting my G-spot so perfectly I can practically see stars, planets, and galaxies.

"Scream my name, baby. I want to hear it."

I stop mid-moan, pulling back just enough to see his face. "Which one baby?" I give a sly smile as he slowly slides in and out, my walls trembling, screaming for that orgasm. I stare at him under hooded eyes and lean close enough that our lips are practically touching, giving that final push by seductively licking my lips. "Mmm...Aleister, please."

And that did it. He slammed into me so hard it triggered my orgasm and I twisted his piercings, sending him into his own earth-shattering climax. Causing me to arch my back and scream out his name in bliss.

He sets me down, and there we are, breathless under the cascade, desperately holding on to each other. After a few moments, he takes a sponge, lathers it up with his masculine body wash. I smile, knowing I would go to sleep smelling just like him. He washes my back, then front, taking his time on the front, caressing my perky nipples and letting the suds slide down my curves with a wide smile on his face. "Watch it, mister, you're setting yourself up for round two." He just laughs.

After rinsing the soap off, I was pleasantly surprised to find him already eager again. I was a little more sore than I would like to admit. I thought about it, but decided against another round. Instead, I positioned him under the shower-head, watching the water cascade over his body.

With my clean clothes still in Digi's room, I had no choice but to sleep naked. I watched him stroll to his side of the bed. I slid in beside him, covered myself with the sheet before laying on him as he put an arm behind his head. He sighs as I get comfortable and I find his hand gently massaging my scalp. The silence was blissful.

What a night, indeed.

Cupid

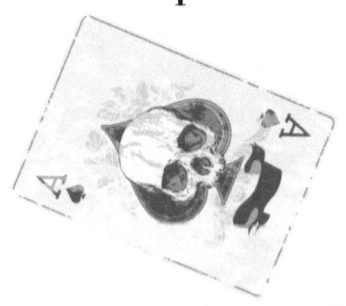

I finally had her. Lost in the throes of the fire lit between us, and she was everything I wanted and more. More than I ever hoped for, her moans drove me insane. Her body, warm and yielding against mine, felt like a dream. The scent of her skin, mingled with my body wash, was intoxicating. This was more than a hope; it was a burning, beautiful reality.

With her hand gently drawing aimless shapes on my chest, a sense of peace settles over me. Enough for me to open up.

"I've been disappearing to my mother's grave. Losing her is the reason I shut down emotionally and I've never opened my heart to anyone. I spend my time talking to her... about you."

Her icy blue eyes meet mine, and she nods before putting her head back on my chest.

"I assumed you were avoiding me, so I spent most of my time at the bar. I didn't want to cramp your style." She shifts up a bit, and I feel her soft breasts slide against my skin. The same ones I had devoured only ten minutes ago. I felt myself stiffen.

I also felt a pang of guilt. I should have never made her feel unwanted or like a burden. I bend down to kiss her forehead. "Far from the truth, I slept miserably without you beside me, and I was mad at myself for letting us drift apart. I kept pumping Digi for information on how you were doing since you two had grown so close."

Her shoulders bob up and down, showing she was laughing. "Digi reminds me of my little brothers, so innocent and cute. I'm not surprised you asked him. We would talk for hours. He has a lot of questions about girls."

He was at that age and we gave him the talk, but it never went further than that. He never openly asked about girls. I suppose it took a girl to get him to see the infinite possibilities. There was a long pause before she continued. "So, why did you leave the bar tonight? You didn't see the hard work I put into the reopening."

I stifled a growl in my chest, recalling what I saw. "You were dancing with that squeaky-clean lawyer guy and you were smiling and laughing. He was making you happy. Why would I take that from you?"

She sits up, covering her amazing set of tits. She knows me well. "He just asked me to dance to celebrate, and I was smiling because it was my favorite song. The people on the dance floor were egging us on, but the moment I saw you, my heart sank because, more than anything, I wanted you to be there. I wanted you to spin me and dance, celebrating this milestone. I know you wanted me to sell the place, but I love it there, having something that's mine. I never had that before. I always relied on someone else. I know I rag on this town, but honestly, I've grown fond of it. The people treat you with respect and are kind, plus you're here." She squeezed my hand, and I brought hers up to kiss softly.

"You made it crystal clear in front of everybody that you stayed because you didn't want to leave me, and I'll be honest, it scared me to death. I never had someone who wanted me for more than my status in the club, among other things." I laughed to break up the seriousness, but she just stared blankly.

Well, I tried.

I pull her back down and closer to me. "I want to tell you what caused me to turn so cold."

She leans up and gives me a soft kiss filled with comfort and attentiveness.

"Go ahead, I'm not going anywhere."

I tell her about what I know about my deadbeat father, which isn't much, the revolving door of men after that and her time with Mr. Wellington.

"I watched my mother, her eyes hollow and her spirit broken, waste away after he tossed her aside like trash, he discarded her like a used condom and yet she still loved him. No one else would ever have her whole heart, not even her own son." I told her about having her committed for her mental state and how she acted upon her return.

She patted my chest. "Your mom just wanted to be loved. It's sad that all these men used her and threw her away, causing cracks in her psyche. You did the right thing by having her committed. I know that was the toughest thing in your life."

How wrong she was. That was one of the easiest decisions.

I sigh, a heavy weight settling in my chest, as I approach the hardest part of her story. "Let me connect the dots between me and Johnny," She shudders. I kiss her forehead, aware of her lingering trauma.

"I don't know what kind of punishment this was, but one day I found my mom straddling Johnny. Sucking his face and practically humping him in the living room. I wanted to believe that maybe, just maybe, he had some soft spot for her and would treat her decently. She was an adult, and I had to let her make her own decisions, but this one, I should have stepped in! It only took eight months before she and Johnny were arguing all the time. She said some girl came to her door and spilled all the details about her and Johnny's steady romps at the nearby motel, including receipts. She knew details about him that only people who had seen him naked could identify. Apparently, he had his dick pierced, something I could have gone without knowing, but it was a dead giveaway that he had been cheating. My mom lost it and kicked the girl out... then went on a rampage, breaking everything in the house. He walked in during her meltdown, called her crazy, and that just made it worse. She focused her rage and emotion at him as she screamed about the girl, about the lies and how he said he would never hurt her, and they'd live a normal life. He countered, telling her he never said that. That she was a fun time and financially supported his addiction. Before he was dealing, he was using. I bet he's using now. No way can he be clean while still selling. The temptation is too great."

I shifted a bit. "Anyway, I came in just as he was breaking up with her. He said he could get sex from anywhere and that he had on the regular and she was just a pathetic loser. Her heart broke, and she ran up the stairs. Before I could turn around, he was already gone. I tried to clean up the signs of their unhealthy relationship while I waited, waited for the wailing to begin, the screaming and I'd be there to pick up the pieces again. But...there was complete silence, and I got a sense of utter dread. Something was wrong this time. I ran up the stairs yelling, Mom! Then I opened her door..."

My breathing hitched, a lump forming in my throat as I neared the toughest part of the story, the words heavy with unspoken pain. "There she was. Lying face down on her bed surrounded by two empty pill bottles and a bottle of vodka clutched in her hand. She combined her antidepressants with sleeping pills and took them with alcohol. I tried, I tried to wake her, but she didn't respond. I called the paramedics and held her while I waited. I screamed at her not this way! And what about me? She opened her eyes once more and whispered that she was sorry and that she loved me. She was dead before they arrived. The combination made a toxic cocktail her body couldn't handle. My mother died because of love and that's why I blame Johnny and all the others. I want them to burn in hell for what they did to her. Watching her die was the hardest thing I had to do. I swore to never allow my heart to be so available to be broken like that again."

As I looked down, Lyric's hand reached out to wipe away a tear that was sliding down my cheek. My tough biker exterior broke. I was a helpless, crying child, missing his mother.

"I'm sorry, so sorry what you had to witness, that she had to suffer because she wanted to be loved. It makes sense now and if you still want something between us, we can take it slow."

I expected her to walk out because of the craziness of why I am the way I am, but she didn't. She said she would wait. Isn't it weird that the roles are reversed? But I look at this little beauty and pull her lips to mine, which turns into a full make-out session. She straddles me, hovering just above my dick, leaning forward. "I will wait for you, if you want me to."

The sound of heavy breathing echoed off the walls. What I wanted was to plunge my rock-hard dick back into her soft cavern that knew how to squeeze me so deliciously. I wanted to pump into her at lightning speed until she cried out in ecstasy. But right now, I need her to know what I really want..."More than anything, baby."

She plants a kiss on me, and suddenly things get hot and heavy.. I kissed her all the way down until I reached my favorite place. All I can focus on are her moans and pants, driving me wild with desire. I am drowning in her, drowning in this girl who finds no fault in me, who will wait. She's perfect, perfect for me.

"There... right there! I'm so close, baby. So close! Oh!" She's screaming into a pillow when then there's a knock on the door.

"Sorry! We'll keep it down." I yell as she laughs behind her hand, trying to keep quiet.

"Yeah, well, that too, but the police are here for Lyric."

That totally kills the vibe when she jumps up to change. I threw her the leggings she had on earlier and one of my long shirts since she decided to not put on a bra. I smile as I can still see the flush on her face.

We walk down to see two uniformed officers in the living room with Jackal and Cheetah.

This can't be good.

Lyric

What could they want with me? Did I serve someone underage? Was the liquor license expired? I had so many scenarios in my head and I still would have never prepared for what they would tell me.

They watch me as I come down the stairs, but they're probably looking at the massive moving boulder behind me. My personal guard dog.

"Good morning gentlemen, seeing as it's like 2 am, what can I do for you?"

They look at each other and grimace before they look at me, trying to see who is going to relay the information. The younger officer steps forward. "Ms. Pullman, there was an incident at your bar shortly after 1:10 am."

My stomach dropped, a cold dread gripping me as tears welled in my eyes, blurring my vision. "W-what? What do you mean? How bad is it?"

I felt my legs weakening and instinctively leaned further back into Aleister for support.

"I'm sorry, but there was a structural fire. The fire crew is currently there trying to extinguish the remaining flames, but it looks to be a total loss."

I reacted before I got some sense. "Take me there now, please!"

I didn't mean to yell, but I couldn't believe it. I had to see it. I had to know.

"Let me take you, sweetheart." I turn to see Aleister grabbing his bike key. I nod while wiping my tears away. He grabs my face. "Hey, listen, it's going to be okay."

I know he's trying to keep me calm, but I'm a fucking wreck.

Cupid

Jesus, it's gone.

The entire building is gone. Reduced to cinders.

The second she was off the bike, she crumpled, knees hitting the dirt road, sobs wracking her body. The acrid stench of smoke, thick and choking, filled her nostrils as hot tears streamed down her face. Her newly found hope burned to ashes, the ashes the firefighters were still hosing down.

It was her dream, and she put so much hard work into it. I watched my baby girl fall apart. The guys followed us because they knew how much she loved that place. They were as heartbroken as me to see her in such a state.

Her wails brought back memories of my mother, and though I tried to comfort her, her grief was overwhelming. The silver lining was that a week earlier she'd put her cash and important documents into a bank safe deposit box; with the police report and insurance, she had the means to rebuild if she wanted.

To be honest, I didn't want her to. I started having different thoughts, of us leaving here, me leaving the club to make her dream of living on the beach come true. Being happy with just the two of us.

We spent about an hour with the cops on scene. "We're sorry this happened, Ms. Pullman. We'll keep in touch with any updates." With a nod, she walked back towards my bicycle.

I wait until she is far enough away. "I want you to look into a girl named Patricia Freeman, but she goes by Trixie. She came by our clubhouse and there was an altercation between her and my girl and she threatened her. I'd put my money on her."

"Anyone else?" I shake my head and walk back, trying to figure out how to console her.

We arrived home at 3:05am; the creak of her shoes broke the silence as she slowly climbed the stairs. I stayed downstairs with the guys. With a frustrated sigh, I ran my hands through my hair, tugging while I paced the room.

"Fuck! Just when everything was settling down, this happened. What do I say to her? I can't imagine how she feels right now. I don't... I don't know what to say."

They all look at me with the same face, a face full of not knowing what to do.

"You need to be there. Just as she has been lying in wait for you to open up." Jackal claps me on my back.

"I shared everything with her tonight. She said she was still willing to wait for me. She's everything to me. I was so stupid for trying to push her away."

"Go up there and console her. We'll figure it out in the morning. Everyone needs to get some sleep. I'll have Digi see if he can find anything in the footage, if he's well enough."

Feeling defeated, I go up the stairs.I can hear her sobs and sniffles. She doesn't even react when I walk in. I shut my door and take off everything except my boxers. I let her stay in her leggings and my shirt and pull her to me.

"W-what am I go-going to do? It's all that I had." Her body wracked in sobs. I continued rubbing her back and kissing her forehead, whispering positive affirmations until she fell asleep.

I was furious; I would bet my life that skanky bitch had something to do with this. I was going to find out and make her pay. I didn't sleep a wink, watching my beautiful girl sleeping peacefully but with a frown on her face, her cheeks stained in dried tears and her clutching my hand tightly.

No need to worry, I'm not going anywhere.

By morning, the news reported about the arson and outlets were trying to get a statement from Lyric, but I told them there would be no interviews.

While downstairs, I fixed her a small breakfast of oatmeal and fruit and brought it up. When I opened the door, she was clutching the pillow in front of her. I set the food down on the nightstand and pulled her towards me. She clung to me, shaking, as if experiencing a panic attack.

"Where were you?"

"Hey, it's okay, I'm here. I went to grab something for you to eat. I thought maybe we'd spend the day in bed and avoid the world for a while. How does that sound?" She gives me a small smile, showing she liked that idea. I place the bowl of oatmeal on the pillow in her lap. I hold another bowl filled with fruit and a bag of granola. I watch her place the fruit and some granola in her bowl. She stirs slowly and then sniffles. "I'm sorry I'm such a drag..." I pull her face in my direction, her eyes filled with unshed tears. "You're not a drag and I'm here for whatever you need, okay?" She nods and eats quietly.

We laid back and watched movies until lunchtime. I brought her up a deluxe chicken Caesar salad and breadsticks that I texted Digi to tell Club to make ahead of time. Hour after hour, her light shined brighter and the sadness slowly faded away. I tried to keep her mood up by choosing comedies and occasionally poking at her side, making her squeal. She'd lace our fingers together and would kiss my hand. She loved the role reversal. Trying to "romance" me instead of the other way around.

Around 2 pm she turns around after spooning since the

last movie. "I wish this were all a dream, a nightmare I could just wake up from. The only saving grace is I have you around. Thank you for trying to cheer me up." She kisses my cheek and I muss her hair. "No problem, kiddo."

Lyric

He's trying his best, he really is, and for that I am thankful. Beneath me, though, is a fire, hot and relentless, burning inside of me; who is responsible for this and why?

I assume it's that trashy ass Malibu Barbie after our last altercation and her threat to "finish this" but she's not bright enough. No, she must be working with someone or there's someone else who wants my place gone.

My gut says Johnny has something to do with this. He's been visibly absent since the bar fight and retaliatory attack. Word is he's been handling business with a new client, moving literal truckloads of crystal meth and ecstasy through the Badlands to California.

Supposedly, his new client is filthy rich, legally owning a top firm and owning a multi-million-dollar mansion high on the hills. Why was he dealing with the likes of a scumbag toad like Johnny beats me.

Another rumor about his absence is that Johnny's new boss wanted to sell the buyer inferior products at the same price, and assigned Johnny to retrieve the cheap merchandise. Which means he wasn't here when my place burned down, but I wouldn't put it past him to pay someone else to do it. Like the STD queen.

I hope to find out what happened soon. Digi was well enough to pull the camera footage from the security company's main drive. I hope somehow... some way we find out who did this.

Unknown

"Johnny, I'm short a goddamn kilo of meth. What gives? You skimming off the top again? The only reason you aren't dead by my hands yet is I need this shipment to the Davila Cartel tomorrow. Lay off the drugs, you fucking cokehead, before you get us all killed trying to short the Cartel. Now go get another fucking kilo!"

The sharply dressed man slammed his hands down on his desk and Johnny jumped up quickly to produce that kilo somehow before tomorrow morning when the Davila family pulled up to his boss's two-story, six-bedroom, four bathroom hacienda style ranch home.

Or one of his homes. He kept a place in New Mexico, Arizona, along the drug trafficking trails to keep an eye out, but his HQ was California, L.A. to be exact.

Almost 30 years ago, he took on his dad's thriving legitimate business, but it wasn't enough. He was money-hungry, trying to live above his means, impress the high-end escorts or sluts he strutted around town with, show them the lavish lifestyle, then fuck their brains out. He wasn't ready to settle down. He loved the fast-paced life of $1200 an ounce Ossetra caviar, wild parties on sports cruiser yachts, French Chateau Petrus Pomerol bordeauxs, and gratuitous sex.

His father, a man of strict rules and traditional values, despised his son's reckless and irresponsible lifestyle, especially since his son was living so comfortably on his money. His father worked hard to build his business and his brand to afford the lifestyle he was in; his son was hanging on his coattails.

So, to punish him, his father placed a stipulation in his will that when he died, the money would go to his first grandchild, not his son. If there was no grandchild, his father would anonymously donate the money to a group of non-disclosed charities.

When he found out his dad's intentions, he was livid. He wanted to kill him, but without an heir that would cause him to lose the money. He stewed in his hatred for his dad.

Desperate, he fathered a child with a girl he met during a drug run from Torréon, Mexico through Chihuahua, through New Mexico on the way to a warehouse distribution center in Las Vegas.

She was an easy lay. He promised her the world to convince her to have sex without protection. He figured she was living in this dead-end town and him being a rich guy from L.A. would spin the perfect fairytale in her mind, and it worked. He even went so far as to take her to L.A. so he could play the family man card to his dad and get his approval, thinking his son was finally settling down.

A façade he used, hoping to collect that money after the child passed on. That was the only loophole to get the money.

His child had to die before he turned 30 to collect his father's millions... that was 29 years ago...

Good thing for him. They never left Van Hollen, New Mexico.

Johnny

Frantically pacing and pulling at his hair, Johnny screamed at his henchmen, "Get Manuel on the phone; I need that kilo!" He couldn't afford another mistake; his drug habit would surely be his demise if he didn't get it together. He went to the back of the warehouse and to his makeshift office.

Stressed, he pulls out a small square mirror and takes a glass vial from inside his jacket pocket, tapping the white powder out in a line. He cuts it with a razor, turning it into an even finer powder before rolling up a dollar bill and snorting the hallucinogen all at once, closing his nostrils so none of it escapes when he exhales.

He groans as he waits for the euphoria to start. He slacks back in his chair and zones out until his door opens.

"So, this is what you fucking do in this entire drug operation. You're just a lackey, an errand boy."

He scoffs as he recognizes that shrill tone. "I don't think I'll take flak from a dejected club whore. What are you doing here, Trixie? You can't get any more inside information. I don't need you anymore."

She confidently strutted in her boldest attire, a black pleather skirt paired with a neon pink tube top, topped with a fuzzy coat and thigh-high boots. She approaches, her tongue darting out to wet her lips in anticipation as she stands before him. She uses her leg to nudge his legs apart before she sinks down to her knees. She pushes the tube top down to reveal her oversized breasts. He licks his lips at the sight of her monumental globes; the skin stretched so tautly you could see the veins.

"You'll always need me. Come on, Johnny... I need a fix.

I'll give you anything you want. I can see you eyeing my breasts. Do you want to touch them?" She pushes his legs further apart and by now the high had hit and he was sporting a raging boner.

He shifts uncomfortably in his chair, his dick pressing painfully against his suit pants. Looking down at her and contemplating. After a few seconds, he grunts, "Don't use your teeth like before and this time. Swallow every drop and I fucking mean it. What good is a whore who doesn't?" He hands her the rest of his vial and there's a gleam in her eye.

"No problem, just promise to fuck me after? It's not fair if only you get off."

"Why is that my problem? Why don't you get your precious Cupid to fuck you?"

She growls and sneers as he chuckles, "Oh yeah, that's right, he's got that pretty little thing to get him off now. She has some soft-looking lips too, almost had them wrapped around my dick. I bet they feel magical. You know what they say about new pussy..." He trails off, knowing he pissed her off.

"That simple bitch isn't his. I am! I'm going to get rid of her and have him all to myself. Besides, he'll never have better pussy than me, isn't that right?"

He didn't answer, didn't want to hurt her feelings at how subpar she was in every way. Besides, why waste a blowjob when the option was there. He grunts and watches her work.

She unzips his pants and his dick pops out with the tip red and throbbing. He hisses as the air hits the sensitive area. She slides her tongue over the head before her lips envelop him. The drugs coursing through his body only heightened his sensitivity, which made her mediocre work decent. "Oh yeah baby, that's it...be the dirty whore that you are."

Cupid

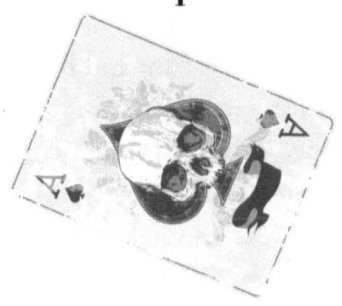

Digi points at the vantage points. "So, there are six cameras installed, one in the office and five surrounding the bar area. I got into the security company's mainframe and retrieved the footage around the time the fire took place. I, uh, also found the footage before you were attacked and what happened to Dave prior. Honestly, Lyric, that footage is pretty..."

"Play it."

I saw the pain reflected in her eyes, a sudden tightening of her mouth. "Sweetheart, I don't think it's a good idea." I try to convince her, but she's as stubborn as I am as she glares at me. She wanted answers. I sigh and signal for Digi, and he starts the recording of her attack on the screen.

I felt like a thermometer in boiling water. I hit a new level of pissed off as I watch that bastard Johnny stalk and prey after Lyric with his sorry ass associates helping intimidate her. She ducks behind the bar in fear after he hits her, then she hurls a bottle at him to keep him a safe distance. He deflects it, and it seems to make him madder.

The worst part is the audio. I heard every disgusting thing that the bastard said.

His threatening words echoed in my ears, igniting a fierce determination to inflict as much pain as I could when the time came. He sparked a demon I haven't seen in a very long time and he was thirsty to be fed. The darkness wanted slivers of Johnny's soul.

I watched as she tried to run, and he brutally pulled her by her hair before hitting her again.

I feel another rage driven blackout coming, and it didn't bode well for Johnny the last time.

And then there it was, the sickening moment. He forced her to her knees. Her sobs, a ragged, wrenching sound, filled the air, thick with fear. He started fiddling with his belt and zipper, then Club and Knox burst in.

I look over, and her lip quivers, a single tear tracing a path down her cheek as she

watches herself, reliving the incident. I hear the punches being thrown and things breaking, hoping it was from their bodies being thrown against literally anything, but I couldn't get that image of her, helpless, out of my mind. I walk away, but not before slamming my fist into the nearest wall. I wanna hurt him badly, torture his soul, then let him die painfully. I walk out into the backyard; I can't deal with this right now.

Lyric

I didn't want him to see me like that, so vulnerable and helpless. He storms out, but before he does; he punches the wall by the kitchen. I yelp as he storms out, so furious. I know he was upset. He felt angry that he wasn't there to help.

My mouth fell wide open to see the damage he caused. The hole was massive and deep. Cheetah whispers to Jackal and they both nod.

"Lyric, sweetie, you should go after him. Only you can calm him down." I am still unsure of what to expect as I follow him out back.

Cupid

This white-hot rage consumes me, leaving me unable to speak or act rationally. It feels like a pressure cooker about to explode. I leaned against the fence on the opposite side of the house, looking out to the mountains, gripping the wooden fence posts tightly. My hand was on fire. I hadn't even surveyed the damage.

I hear the familiar sound of the back door. I choked up, couldn't even turn around. I knew it was her.

Her tiny silhouette stood next to me, and I shook my head in anger. "I should have been there! To protect you! He could have, he wanted to... hurt you! I..."

Her hand wraps around my injured hand's arm. She turns me to face her. I rub her cheek with my thumb and as her eyes close to relish in my touch; the tears fell.

It hurt her to see me so angry, but I was after revenge for her and my mother. She gently takes my injured hand. "Come on, we need to treat this before it gets infected," he said, his voice hushed, pointing to the deep gash oozing blood. She rubbed the area under it to calm me.

I look at her. "I'm sorry."

She shakes her head. "Nothing to be sorry for. Come on, caveman, let me bandage you up. Nurse Lyric is on duty."

She gets a chuckle out of me this time. She's one sexy ass nurse and I can't wait to reverse the role and play her doctor, her sexy naked doctor. She pulls me back into the house and while she tends to me, I review only the fire footage this time.

"Hey, rewind that back. That person looks familiar."

Unknown

"So, you're telling me that sexy little tart is..."

Johnny nods, "Yeah, just recently, too. Actually, I'm not sure it's official, but the bastard is protecting her because she's staying at their clubhouse. Dillon confirmed that when he met her there about the bar."

"I wish you would have told me that before I strolled into that bar. I could have taken her then and he would have gladly given up his life for hers."

Johnny steps forward towards his desk and sits down. "I don't think it would have been that easy, especially with me involved, and once he finds out who you are..."

The man swirls his scotch on the rocks and grins. "He didn't figure it out before and it'll be too late by the time he figures it out now. Get that shipment to Tomasa and ensure the freight from Oaxaca, then we can take a trip back to Van Hollen to... tie up some loose ends."

Lyric

I let out a long, pained groan, a testament to my frustration. "I know you're trying Cheetah, but I'm just not that great a shot. I'll never be as good as you." I hold the gun down to my side and look at him, defeated.

"I'm not asking you to be me, honey, *nobody* can be me. I want you comfortable enough to shoot a gun. If push comes to shove, I want you to pull that trigger confidently. You're doing better than when we started.You didn't hit one can the first day. Now you're averaging seven out of ten cans, so back to it, Trigger. Maybe we'll get you nicknamed after all." He chuckles, causing me to. I know his intentions are pure and so I take a deep breath, aim, and shoot at the ten cans perched on the fence.

Ping ping ping

Three in a row! I never did three in a row before! I jumped up and down, but he only pointed towards the rest of the cans, gesturing for me to focus.

Ping ping miss

Dammit!

My shoulders slump and he tsks. "Don't worry about what you miss. Keep going. If someone were shooting at you, they wouldn't stop because they missed. Come on."

I inhaled slowly and knocked off the last four. That earned me a high five.

"See there, nine out of ten, your best one yet. Tomorrow, we'll try moving targets." He takes the gun to clean and pats me on the back. Of course, Cheetah was the natural choice to teach me to shoot. He learned to shoot when he was twelve, and four years later he was beating contestants three times his age.

I rebelled at first but after Cupid saw the tape and how helpless I was; he wasn't taking no for an answer. He even threatened to put me on sexual punishment. Can you believe that?! I was a spoiled princess; I'll be damned if he takes his dick from me!

Just the thought of Cupid's arrow had me weak in the knees and ready to go.

That gives me an idea.

Huh... tonight is going to be quite fun.

Cupid

I spent the last hour in our makeshift gym in the garage opposite where we park our bikes, while I heard the gunshots of Lyric learning to be comfortable shooting, I needed to have some peace of mind if I can't be there to help her.

I spent 15 minutes wailing on the heavy bag. Sweat stung my eyes, the leather's scent thick in the air, a counterpoint to the dull thud-thud-thud of my fists. Each blow, aimed precisely where Johnny's head would be, a precursor to brutal, final impact. The heavy metal music only amplified the violence of each hit as I recalled the assault until utter exhaustion set in.

I sat heavily, gasping for air, the cool water a welcome shock as I drank. A damp chill clinging to my soaked clothes, the smell of a simmering stew tantalizing the air. Dinner, I hoped, was almost ready.

"Yo, Cupid, dinner's done!"

"Alright Knox, I'm coming."

I walk in and head up to take a quick shower. I sigh as I peel off my sweat-drenched tank top. I toss it and my shorts in the hamper.

The heated water felt so good on my throbbing aching muscles I could've stayed in there forever. Reluctantly, I step out and wrap a towel around my waist, air drying my upper half. I stand in front of the mirror and take some time to trim my beard. Don't get me wrong, I love my beard and she does, too. I like to keep it neat and clean.

Besides, I don't want it to irritate her sensitive skin when I'm feasting on her sweetness. Satisfied, I pull my hair up in a man bun and I flick off the light, open the door, and stop in my tracks.

Fuck meeee...my little vixen is not playing fair.

There my little kitten lies in my bed, wearing nothing but a tiny black silk slip and robe.

Only two thoughts are running through my mind at this very moment, due to lack of blood circulation:

Did she pack that or buy it for me? And two, I think I can prop up this towel with just my dick.

A low growl rumbled in my throat as she sat up, arms rigid, her breasts straining against the smooth, silken fabric, almost overflowing. A fingertip traced her lip, a soft, barely audible *click* as her teeth gently nipped it.

"Hi." Her voice, sultry with desire, beckoned. She gestured towards the dresser, then mentioned dinner. Hopefully, she didn't go down in that dress.

I raise my brow and she sighs. "No, I didn't wear this downstairs. It's only for you." She pulls her gown up a bit while sitting with her legs underneath her.

She stared at me. "What?"

I could see she was wondering why I was staring at her. Did I not like the gown, and why was I not making a move to devour her?

"Nothing darlin'. You look absolutely...wow. You have no idea what you do to me."

She giggles, sending a fresh wave of heat through me and I swear I'm even harder, if that's possible. She sinks back against the soft, yielding pillows, the scent of her perfume–a subtle blend of vanilla and something floral, girly–filling the air.

"I want you to take me," She pleaded, her voice thick with need. She leans forward to shrug the robe off her shoulders, letting it rest on her elbows before she leans back.

I slowly crawl onto the bed, planting gentle kisses on her delicate toes before moving up her body. Each kiss sends shivers down her spine, her chest rising and falling rapidly with each breath. As soon as my fingers touch her inner thigh, she jumps in anticipation. Skipping her pussy, my favorite spot, I trace a path from her navel upward, disregarding my second favorite spot, her nipples. By the time I reach her lips, she's pouting in a mix of frustration and agony.

"Now, what's with the face?" I knew I just wanted to see her squirm, and she did. Her hand brushed over her left breast and rested between her legs. She bit her lip, as I suspect that she's trying to relieve her own need. I pull her hand and kiss her fingertips, tasting the familiarity of her sweetness on her fingers.

My naughty, naughty kitten.

I guide her onto her back, the lust crystal clear in her eyes. Her slip, now gathered under her bra, revealed a glimpse of a matching tiny thong.

Am I drooling? Because fuck me.

She purrs. "You trimmed your beard?" While tugging, I didn't think she'd notice.

Touché, my sweetest Lyric.

"Just a bit. I'm impressed you noticed."

"I tug on it constantly and there's less to pull on. Of course I could tell. I use it to pull you forward, like now..."

I fall forward, but my forearms absorb the impact, not her small frame. She pulls my arms, making me collapse onto her; she sighs under my weight.

My face nestled between her breasts, skin like warm silk. The scent of honey and a whisper of lavender filled my senses. I kissed the sweet hollow, tasting the sun-warmed sweetness of her skin. I push the silken straps to the side, revealing her breasts. I gently pull the fabric away, the soft fabric cool against my fingertips. One nipple, already peaked, I take into my warm mouth, the other I tease with a feather-light touch, its delicate skin tingling under my caress.

"Baby..." She gasps and arches her back; her fingers pull my hair loose from the bun so she can run her fingers through and pull to her heart's content. It makes me growl before I bite down lightly on her nipple, causing her to hiss and pull her knees up. I switch, making sure each receives the attention it deserves. I don't think she realizes it, but she's more sensitive on one than the other. I've made her come by concentrating on it and twisting the other.

Her mewls are getting louder as I make my way south.

I swear she tastes even sweeter every time, already soaked by the time I taste her. Her body responds to me as she twists and turns until I wrap my arms around her hips to keep her in place. "You always try to run. When are you going to stop trying?"

"It, it feels too good, baby. I'm so sensitive to you... oh, I'm..."

She grips tighter, signaling her climax, so I don't let up

until I'm tasting her all over me. My eyes watch hers roll to the back of her head.

"I hate you, smug bastard."

I crawl back up to her. "There's that firecracker that cussed me out. Funny thing, I don't know if you know, but when he smacked your ass, and you growled, that's when I knew I was in trouble."

"And here I thought you didn't even notice until I interfered."

"Oh, I noticed, because I was staring at your ass when you turned around and walked away myself, but I was there on club business."

"Some business venture that turned out to be! Almost got yourself killed..." She looked away angrily.

I felt her shudder beneath me, so I kissed her forehead to calm her.

"My guardian angel saved me, even though she's feisty and sometimes stubborn."

"Excuse me? *I'm* the stubborn one? Right..."

I lay my head on her chest as she runs her fingers through my hair. My arms are situated under her arms. We sat in comfortable silence. I listened to her heartbeat, a slow and steady rhythm at first, until I noticed it pick up. I looked into her smiling face. "You're not done yet. That was only the appetizer; now, let's move on to the main course." The words hung in the air with delicious promise.

I knelt in front of her, the sound of our heavy breaths filling the room. I gently slid her smooth legs up and around my waist, feeling the anticipation building between us. In that perfect position, I could plunge into her so deep.

"Oh!" I feel her body quiver beneath me as I take my time, teasing her with each deliberate movement. She digs her nails into me, and I feel a jolt that shoots up my spine. At that moment, our eyes meet.

"Aleister, please." I sped up, grinding into her, and feeling her constrict and pulse around me. I licked the pad of my thumb and pressed it against her clit, moving in fast circles. I watched and felt her get wetter, then applied more pressure. She immediately screamed and convulsed around me.

I lost control. She felt so damn good, pumping at a furious speed until I got close and barely finished on her stomach, I think. I go into the bathroom to get a warm towel and clean her up.

She looked at me strangely as I handed her the towel "Why do you always do that?"

"What?"

"You always decide to pull out."

I could feel that uncertainty creep up and I think she did, too.

I froze with fear.

Lyric

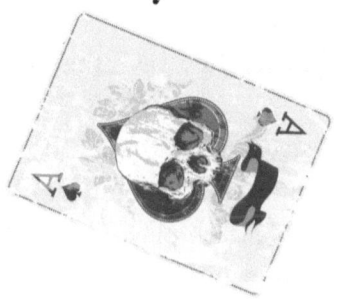

He's clamming up again.

Why do I even try? Okay, let's try to make the situation a little less awkward.

"Never mind, it doesn't matter, really." A shaky chuckle failed to mask the tightness in my throat—a suffocating, bitter lump. The taste of unshed tears pricked my eyes, blurring the already hazy room.

I had to face facts. It hadn't been that long, and we weren't even official yet. At best, we were friends with benefits and that hurt deep in my heart. Even the thought of it was like pulling my heart through a meat grinder. I turn over and wrap myself in the blanket, trying to will myself to sleep, to avoid the soul-crushing awkwardness.

He slides in beside me, but doesn't pull me into him, and turns off the light. I let the tears fall silently. I'd fallen too hard, too fast.

Hours later...

The tossing and turning revealed the unsettling reality

beside me. A cold, unfamiliar stiffness permeated between us, not the warmth I was used to. The silence was heavy, punctuated only by the frantic thumping of my heart. The bitter taste of unrequited love coated my tongue; a painful, suffocating weight settled on my chest. His inability to love felt like a physical blow, each silent breath a stark reminder of the chasm between us.

I get it, I do, but as they say, 'the heart wants what it wants...'

I could barely sleep. I cried silently with my thoughts keeping me up. My mind had given me nothing but negative thoughts, and I was in a dark place. Had I been lying on his chest, I could have used his heartbeat to soothe my racing thoughts.

But I didn't even know if he wanted to touch me or be touched and here I am at 5am staring at the man who is unintentionally breaking my heart. A sob broke out before I could muffle it, and I ran to the closest refuge, his bathroom, to drown it out with the sound of running water.

I sat against the sink cabinet with my knees pulled up and let my world and expectations follow that water down the drain.

Cupid

I relapsed... bad.

I should have spoken up, but she shut down after I stood there saying nothing. I listened to her heartbroken sobs; the sound echoing in my ears, and guilt gnawed at me. No amount of water could drown out her crying.

I keep fucking up and worse; I keep hurting her. I dress

quickly and head out to think. I can't see her heartbroken face, I just can't.

As I storm out, Jackal notices my frustration and follows me out. To avoid talking, I walk faster.

"Hey, Cupid! Don't you ignore me, son."

I let out a frustrated sigh, stopping at the barn door. My anger boiled over, and I slammed my fist against it, hurting myself more than the wood. I deserve it; I deserve to feel pain.

"Hey, what's going on with you? Why are you out here boxing with no gloves? Talk to me."

His dad-voice emerges to coax me to talk. I still can't face him. He'll know instantly. I let my shoulders slump and the weight of the world crush me.

"I'm a complete fuckup, boss. I can't even tell her I like her, that I care for her, that I--"

He pats my shoulder. "Stop beating yourself up."

"Why not?! I deserve it! We had such a wonderful night... and I mean an amazing night of passion..."

"I think we all know that. The walls are thin in the house."

Embarrassing...

"Sorry. She surprised me in my room in the sexiest little number..."

He quickly holds up his hand. "No more detail I've come to love her like a daughter."

"See, even you've fallen for her and can say it. I choked last night, and I listened to her cry. It sounded so much more painful this morning. I'm such a goddamn screw-up! I just need to think."

"Let's go, then." I raise my brow at him as he suits up for the ride.

"We all know where you go, Eros, and it may benefit you from hearing another parental opinion. Besides, I haven't visited up there in a while and I can visit my own angel."

Having no energy left for a fight, I got on my motorcycle; the smell of gasoline and exhaust filled the air as we made our way to the cemetery.

Lyric

I trudge back to Digi's room to change; I'm done with feeling like this, so I start packing. I know I look a mess, unkempt, bloodshot eyes and tears keep slipping from my eyes. I get everything packed and slip downstairs. I try to leave without seeing anyone but...

"Lyric? Where are you going?" Spinning around, I caught sight of Cheetah. I felt a hot tear roll down my cheek. I wiped it away angrily.

"I-I'm going to stay at the hotel. Please, spare me the lecture about how much he cares. I'm at my heart's emotional limit."

The guys all gathered in the room after hearing my raised voice and harsh tone. I felt so grateful to these guys who protected me. I felt loved by them, but it's *his* love in particular that I want.

"Look, I appreciate everything you guys have done, but I can't be here anymore. I need to figure out what's next for me and it's clearly not what I want, so I need to think about what's best for me... not who. When the dust has settled, come visit me, okay?"

I only get a room full of silent nods, but Digi is clearly the most heartbroken. I hug him and hand him my information.

"Don't be a stranger, okay?" He squeaks out a yes and I see the unshed tears. I take my bag and walk out without another word.

Time to figure out a plan...and drown myself in liquor. I want to forget that I ever knew Aleister "Cupid" McElroy!

Unknown

"So, boss, how does this work again? I mean, if you only get the money after you kill your kid, why didn't you, I don't know, drown him when he was a baby or something, call it an accident?"

"Easy, my dad would have known. He would have paid for an investigation and autopsy. He knows how hungry I am for the inheritance. But now he's in his 70s, he hasn't got the energy to waste. Plus, the kid's mom was still alive back then and now that she wasn't. I can execute without interference."

He taps his $500 fountain pen against the antique cherry wood Astoria Grande Makenzie Executive desk in his equally lavish study. They had just completed their last job with no hiccups and were brainstorming how to get his inheritance.

"Once my kid is out of the picture, I'll contact Manuel to make an undetectable poison and take my dad out. Then I get the $35 million to myself... and of course, I'll pay you a service fee IF you can get me the girl."

"I'll deliver her to you, then we can have a good time." Johnny moans to his sick, perverse thoughts.

His boss swings around in his seat to face Johnny. "And what makes you think I don't want that pretty little thing to myself?"

Lyric

I put myself up in a really luxurious hotel room for the week. It was the equivalent to a honeymoon suite, but without all the happiness and joy. No, it was just me, myself, and I, oh, and a broken heart. The suite is bigger than my original place. I drop my bags and look around. I walked to the desk for the room service menu; all this anxiety makes you want to eat your feelings.

"Room Service, can I take your order?"

"Hi, can I get the veggie burger, fries, and a slice of chocolate cake? Room 311, thank you."

I started running the bath; my neck and shoulders were incredibly tense from stress. I was lucky it was a Jacuzzi; those strong jets would have me relaxed in minutes—physically, anyway.

Twenty minutes later, there's a knock on my door.

"Room service."

I open and a young lad pushes the cart in and sets the trays on the kitchen counter. I tip him $20. "Thank you, sir." He leaves me with a delicious dinner, but first my bath and this bottle of vodka from the bar.

Cupid

It's beautiful, as always, up here. Jackal goes to spend some time with Paige, and I visit mom. I shake my head, "Boy, you raised a real screw up, mom. I can't even express my emotions like an adult. I don't know how much more she can take, and I don't want to lose her."

You're stronger than your past, my sweet boy...

I look around. It sounds like, "Mom?"

Let the pain go. I'm at peace.

"I don't know if I can! I miss you."

Open your heart. I'm always with you.

I looked at her headstone and the wind picked up, swirling the leaves, freshly cut grass, and floated away. I felt an overwhelming calm over me.

Later, gazing out at the lake, Jackal sits beside me. It's hard to look tough sitting on the ground in jeans and leather.

"Did you get some insight?"

I look to the sky, "Yeah, nothing like a mother's wisdom." He claps my back and we get up to head home.

Once there, we parked our bikes and headed inside. The living room was filled with the hushed silence of grief. Everyone sat somberly until they looked up, their expressions causing a wave of unease to wash over me.

"Are you happy now?! She's gone...you broke her heart so much that she left! Why did you take her from me?!?!"

Digi was always the quiet one, the last person I would expect to be in my face, but he is and he's on the verge of tears when Club pulls him back.

I hear my heart break as I realize what he just said, and I look at Blondie for confirmation. "She left about an hour and a half ago with her stuff, and said she was going to the hotel."

No...

I have to see for myself. I went to my room and sure enough not a trace of her ever being there. Then I went to Digi's room and nothing, even the top bunk had been made. She was nowhere to be found except the lingering scent of her on my sheets. I stomp back down the stairs, obviously frustrated.

"Fuck! Tell me exactly where she is. Blondie, Club?" They shrug their shoulders. "She only gave that specific info to Digi." I grit my teeth because I know he's going to overreact.

I turn toward him slowly, and he shakes his head. Now I've got the kid by several inches and at least 100 pounds. I could just manhandle the information out of him, but he's my brother and I know he's just protecting her.

He bolted upstairs, slamming and locking the door before I had a chance to say anything.

Dammit!

I pull at my hair while pacing, trying to think, think of what I can do or say.

I snap my fingers. "There's only one hotel..." I turn to go after her, but I'm stopped by Cheetah.

"I saw her earlier, and she was really upset. Maybe you should give her some time. I know you want to be with her, but what she wants is so much more. Can you give her that? Can you even tell her how you feel?"

Wow, that hurt. It was a real gut punch because I wasn't even sure I could do it when the time came. What did I have to offer her?

With all hope gone, I went to my room and spent the night basking in the scent of a girl who deserves much more.

Lyric

I spent some time at the pool today to get out of that room and my never-ending funk. I am glad I packed a simple two-piece black bikini. I bought one of those big floppy hats and a trashy romance mystery novel to read as I was sunbathing.

I found myself envious of the passersby who were only here as a pit stop on their way home or to a dream destination they've always wanted to go to.Their destinations might have included the California sand dunes, northern wine country, or a lengthy Colorado ski trip, the possibilities were endless. Those possibilities pass my mind obsessively now, with the money I could start over anywhere I wanted.

I set my book down and lay my head back and rest as the sun warms my skin, giving me that sun-kissed glow I needed. I order a Mai Tai and sigh deeply as I enjoy the tropical-like environment. It's my version of the beach and after all I've been through, I'll take even this version of it.

"Lyric? Is that you?"

I moved my hat to see a dark figure because the sun was

directly in front. I shadow my eyes and finally see, "Dillon? Hey, what are you doing here?"

He sits in the chair next to me. He's casually dressed in khaki shorts and a white button-down. It's a good look for him instead of that stuffy suit.

"Well, since the bar burned down, they sent me back to survey the damage and make sure it wasn't malicious."

He looks at me forlornly, feeling guilty at what he was implying. "It's okay, Dillon. You're just doing your job. I would never burn down a place I grew to love, and the police haven't updated me yet to potential suspects."

I catch him eyeing my bathing suit before he clears his throat. "So, why are you at the hotel? I thought you were staying with that big biker guy and his gang."

Not even one day of reprieve, huh?

"It's a club, not a gang. They were just keeping me safe, and I have relieved them of their services, nothing more."

He chuckles as he sips his beer. "Who are you trying to convince, me or yourself? I saw your face light up when he showed up at the bar and quickly fall when he left without so much as a word. He obviously thought there was something going on between us, and I'm just glad he didn't rip me in two. He's the essence of a scary biker dude."

We share a laugh. "Yeah, well, no need to worry about it now. That, whatever it was, is over." I couldn't help but sigh a bit.

"So, is it okay for a friend to ask a friend out so soon? Like bowling or the movies? Sounds like you could use some cheering up. Come on..."

He smirks, and I notice his smile. It's perfect, but there's no light behind it. It was forced. I still feel the blush on my cheeks.

That's enough Mai Tai's for today.

"Can I think about it? How long are you here for?"

"Another week. Please consider it." He takes my hand and kisses it. "I'll see you around. You have my number." He waves goodbye and disappears back into the hotel.

I smile inwardly as I throw myself back into my novel. My money is on the bitter, jealous sister who was written out of the will.

Unknown

"Fuck! There's a goddamned second part to the stipulation I hadn't seen until now." As he reads over the paperwork and slams his hand down, waking up Johnny.

Johnny rubs his face and leans forward.

"What is it, boss?"

"It says... he automatically gets the money on his 30th birthday, whether or not my dad is alive. Fuck! He's 29 now, I'm running out of time! Tell Dillon to speed up the process. I need the Princess sooner than I thought to get my son here to kill him.

Lyric

I was relaxing with my book in the dimly lit living room; the pages rustling softly in my hands, when a soft knock echoed at my door. I hadn't ordered room service, so I didn't know who it was. Cautiously, I approach the door; they knock again, startling me.

"L-lyric, it...it's m-me!"

I knew that squeaky voice and he sounded so sad. I realized his stutter was based on emotion or turmoil. The more upset he was, the worse it got. I opened my door and immediately hugged him. "Digi! I missed you and it's only been a day. How are you?"

I pull him in and close the door. His leather vest hangs off him so awkwardly because he's scrawny, but I bet he'll bulk up in a few years. He hits the gym like the others do.

Settling onto the worn sofa, I notice his attempt at a small smile, a flicker of something. "I-it's... terrible without yo-you. I lost my temper the moment he stepped in the house. I just started screaming about how he let you down and it was because of him you left. I wanted to get it through his thick skull how much he messed up! I ran upstairs and never came back down until I came to see you."

I pulled out the menu. "You must be hungry then. Let's order some snacks, okay?" He agrees as I call room service and order a buffet of food. He may be skinny, but the kid can eat a ton, I've seen it.

Now, I was curious. "Digi, do they know where you are?"

He shakes his head. "I didn't want to talk to them. I slipped out when a few of them took a ride to handle some club business."

I pick up the phone again and dial the clubhouse, looking at his concerned face.

"Black Aces, this is Blondie."

"Hey, Blondie, it's Lyric," I heard his breathing hitch. "I just wanted to say that Digi is safe with me. He'll spend the night here, okay?"

"Y-yeah, okay. Umm, it's good to hear from you, Lyric. Take care of yourself, sweetie."

"Thanks."

I hang up and he's smiling more. "You just wanted a sleepover." His smile was now a full grin.

"I had to get out of there. I know you don't want to hear this, but Eros is being sulky and keeps pestering me for your location, but I refused to tell him.

"Eros?"

"Yeah, sometimes we cut him a break from the Cupid silliness. We call him by the Greek god of love instead."

"Oh." *The irony.*

There's an awkward silence. He stands, taking in the luxurious room; plush carpets, the four-poster bed, a view of the mountains, and murmurs, "This is really nice, like a honeymoon suite."

I get up to grab drinks and he walks out to the balcony. It may be a small town, but beyond that were the pristine hills before the snow-capped mountains. It really was a stunning view.

"Lyric, can I ask you a question?" His curious nature was showing, but I already knew the subject. Maybe talking it out would help. If not, I can always drown myself in dessert and booze.

"Of course."

He steps back inside, sitting on the barstool across from me. He grabs his drink, tapping the surface.

"Did you... or were you, uh, in love with him?"

Et tu, Digi?

"Love is a complex emotion. It's hard to express love so simply. And we were never official, so..." I shrug my shoulders.

He holds his hand up and smiles. "But that's not what I asked. You've been like a sister to me and you've been around long enough for me to see it. You're in love with him, it's in your eyes, your face lights up and I've never seen him smile or be so openly affectionate. I don't see why it has to be this way!"

He gets up, scraping the chair against the floor before he plops down on the couch, biting his nails. His leg bounces until I sit next to him and rest my hand on his knee to stop him.

He looks at me, "You know I had a dream that you two would move away to a nice place and that you would take me with you to live a normal life. I guess it was stupid to think it could ever happen. I wanted a normal life and family. I'm tired of being abandoned." He squeaks out the last part.

In that moment, I realized this affected not only me. We had grown so close and for him; it felt like his dream of a family. I forget how young he is and everything he's already gone through. He was in a motorcycle club group filled with rough, gruff men, but he himself was just a sweet boy.

"Oh sweetie, I'm sorry. This is just so complicated beyond if I love him."

He sniffles with his head down. "Well, do you love me? You said I was like a little brother to you because I've grown to love you as my sister and like a mom."

"Of course, I love you! You're the sweetest boy I've ever met. You're smart and funny, you love helping others, and I know you're going to do amazing things one day."

He looks at me and surprises me with a hug. I let the hug go on for however long he needs. A minute later, he releases me.

"I'm sorry. I really needed that. I wish you could work it out."

I huff, "Well, it's not me who has the difficulty in expressing my feelings..."

"Are you sure? Because you still haven't answered my question."

He was right; I hadn't, and that was the first step. Was *I* even ready to say it out loud?

Cupid

"Would ya stop sulking, jeez, if you're so damn broken up about it, why don't you just tell her. Man the hell up, Cupid. You're named after the epitome of all that is love. Do you know why we gave you that for a club name? Not to rag on you. No, it's because beyond that tough 'fuck it all' exterior, we all know you have the biggest heart and you're protecting it, so you don't get hurt."

I stare Blondie down, my eyes blazing, a furnace of anger. The air crackles with unspoken tension. I didn't need this shit. Everyone avoids me, their whispers an icy reminder to the dull ache in my chest.

Digi is with her, where I should be. I got up and went to my bike. I told myself I needed the breeze on my back, but that's not the truth.

I needed to see her, even if I had to knock on every damn door in the hotel!

Lyric

"Digi, you remember Dillon? We're going to go to the movies and then lunch, okay?"

"L-like a... date?" He said defensively.

I could see how he felt about it. But it wasn't a date, just a friend cheering up another friend. Dillon had texted me before I went to bed and spent the time making me laugh until I agreed. It's harmless.

"Umm, I guess so." I could feel the judgement in his eyes. He wanted his brother and me together. I suppose I did too, but I would not sit and wait or hold my breath.

I cleared my throat. "I'll be back soon. Order whatever you like, it's on me!" I tried to joke, but he just looked away. I'll have to deal with that later.

It's just a friendly date, plus I needed to take my mind off of certain people.

"You look gorgeous." Dillon says as he lets me pass by to get on the elevator. I felt the blush rise on my cheeks. I wore a floral dress and wedge sandals, my hair swept up. I grabbed a red sweater for the inevitable chilly movie theater. He chose some sappy rom-com, but I chalked it up to trying to cheer me up.

After the sap fest, we walked out of the theater to the warm afternoon sun. He pointed towards the cozy bistro nestled on the hotel's corner, the patio umbrellas beckoning us from the sidewalk. The temperature is bearable, even with the light breeze.

"Are you still cold? We can go inside. I thought we could enjoy the scenery."

I look up from the menu. "No, this is fine. Do you know what you want?"

The deep rumble of a motorcycle sent shivers down my spine, goosebumps erupting across my arms. I hear it coming my way and I try not to react while he's talking, to seem interested. I see the bike and my eyes follow it straight to my hotel.

Holy hell! What is he doing?

He hops off and sets his helmet down and pulls his hair up. He knows I love it pulled up unless we're in bed where I love to run my hands through it, yank it to add a little pain to the pleasure.

In his leather vest and jeans, he commanded everyone's attention. Women approached, but he waved them off, heading into the hotel.

"Umm, Dillon, I'll be right back. Stay here."

That's all I need is for Aleister to see me anywhere near another man, especially Dillon. He would go nuclear.

I walk into the hotel, but don't see him. I went to the front desk. "There was a tall biker guy that just came in. Where did he go?"

The girl's eyes widened, and she seemed overwhelmed by my sudden appearance and unexpected question. "Uh, I sent him to the room he requested, 311. He said he was her husband. That they had a fight, and he was here to apologize."

Clever man.

"Oh no, did I make a mistake? I can call security to have him escorted off the premises! I'm so sorry, Miss!" She was upset, shaking, and on the verge of tears.

"Oh no. He just surprised me. He's right, we had a fight. I guess it's kiss-and-make-up time. Don't worry, everything's fine, thank you."

I hear him and Digi already, even before exiting the

elevator. I see him, his hands pressed against my door. "Digi, please, open the door. I need to see her." I'm backed against the wall as I sidestep closer.

"No! I won't let you hurt her anymore! You don't love her, and I need her..." His voice cracked and my heart broke. "She's like a mother to me. She makes me feel wanted."

At that moment, I paused. Aleister's head drops, a heavy sigh escaping his lips as his open hand slides across the cool, smooth surface of the door.

"I know. She's brightened my life, too. I don't want to lose her either, buddy. I came to make it right."

He turned his head, his jaw dropping slightly as he stared at me in disbelief. "Kitten?"

I take my key out and nudge past him to open the door. I leave it open for him to follow, and he does.

"What do you want, *Eros*?" There's sarcasm in my tone. He stops short and looks at Digi.

Digi stares back, shrugging his shoulders. I lean against the kitchen island. He rubs his neck. "Digi, can you give us a minute?"

Digi looks to me for confirmation. "It's okay." He walks into my bedroom and closes the door.

He approaches me, his hands reaching for me, craving my touch, but I hold my hand up. "Really? Do you think anything physical is a good idea? Besides, I walked away from my friendly date to see what you are up to, so what do you want, Aleister?" I cross my arms. He better say the right thing.

Cupid

God, when she says my name, I want to do things to her, but she's mad. Wait. Did she say she was... on a date?

"On a date? With who?"

She turns to grab a glass. "Does it really matter at this point? It's irrelevant."

"It isn't irrelevant. Have you moved on already?"

She sighs loudly. "Jesus, Aleister, it's one friendly date to cheer me up, that's all. I was tired of feeling sad and alone. This isn't what you came here to hear. So, what is it? I need to get back."

She was acting petty, and it kinda stung. She couldn't wait to go back to have a good time with someone else. I was losing her and all because I couldn't...

Well, it was now or never...

Lyric

I saw his eye twitch, a single, barely perceptible spasm, when I mentioned my date, and his knuckles whitened as his grip tightened when I said I had to leave. If I would have told him it was Dillon, he would have pummeled him into a bloody pulp. He never trusted him from the start.

He is insanely jealous and territorial, but that's not my problem. "Well?" I said, annoyed he wasn't saying anything. I shift my weight and watch his gaze cover my entire being. I feel the heat grow between us.

He rubs the back of his head and lets out a long, weary sigh. "Fuck baby, I don't know how to start."

I relaxed a bit. He's trying. I hold my hand out and offer an olive branch. His large hands wrap around mine and he kisses it, a look of relief on his face. Then he does the unthinkable. He drops to his knees in front of me.

"Lyric, sweetheart, I'm so sorry. I don't deserve someone as perfect as you. You are the sweetest, kindest, gentlest soul I know. You're spunky, feisty, and can hold your own. I need someone who can put me in my place and put my broken pieces together. I need you, kitten."

His strong arms wrap around my waist, squeezing tight. He deeply inhales the scent of my perfume. A sharp, clean scent filling the air between us. A painful lump swells in my throat, a hot, prickly sensation rising, threatening to spill tears. I fight to maintain control, to not appear weak. Then, his eyes meet mine and it's like we're back at the beginning, the raw vulnerability of day one returning. The sound of his unspoken words, finally heard in the silence, is a balm to my soul. I needed to hear him say it.

"You need me?"

He nods his head. "I need you, baby."

"You want to be with me?"

He stands and places his hands on my face. "Absolutely. I want to whisk you away on my bike to the beach or live in a cabin far away from the world. Just you and me."

Well, that did it.

Tears shed. It's like that damn cheesy rom-com I was forced to watch. I can only cry and hug him, my throat too sore to talk.

He separates us to look me in the eye with a slight smile. "Lyric, I love... oof!"

His eyes went wide with shock, his body jerking forward violently before sliding down and hitting the floor with a thud.

"Aleister? ALEISTER! Oh... Oh God!!!"

He's motionless on the floor, and I notice something sticking out from the back of his vest. It's a... dart? My mind is racing with so many thoughts that I couldn't comprehend anything going on. I just needed him to wake up.

"Don't worry your pretty little head. It's just a professional grade tranquilizer to keep your guard dog at bay."

Dillon stood there, gun drawn, the other hand already holstering his weapon to his waist. His face, in his true form, was a mask of evil intent. Twisted into a smirk as he revealed his true nature. He wasn't a friend, not anymore.

"But this one here isn't a tranquilizer gun, so you better behave and do what I say. I don't think my client would appreciate me injuring his prized possession, but I will, if you disobey."

I don't know what to say. My whole body is shaking and the man I love is unconscious on the floor.

Dillon closes the door, that we left slightly ajar, softly. "I guess I should explain what's going on here. You see, I was paid a lot of money to use you as a lure to get lover boy there to my client's place."

I look down; his chest rises and falls. He's breathing, but unconscious. I pull out the dart and roll him onto his back. Feeling for a heartbeat, I'm relieved to find a steady thump against my hand.

I squeeze his cheeks together. "Hey, stay with me. I need you, too. Okay, baby?" I place my lips to his cold, unresponsive ones to kiss my Prince Charming awake. Like Sleeping Beauty, but to no avail. That's when the tears clouded my vision of my sleeping giant.

Why is he doing this to us?

Dillon's on the phone. "Yeah, well, I thought we'd just take her as bait, but the big ape showed up! So tell Johnny to bring his men. We have to get the big oaf out of here through the back exit."

My mind is racing as fast as my heart and all I can do is

cry and touch his face, tug at his beard like he loves me to do when we're just lounging lazily.

Please, baby... wake up... please...

Then a door opens in the room. I forgot about...

"Hey, Lyric, I was playing Space Invaders with my headphones on. I heard a thud, are you o..."

Dillon spins around and shoots toward the voice.

Bang

And I watch his innocent eyes go wide in shock as he stumbles, then falls with a soft thud, the silence deafening as my mind went completely blank, and I rushed over to him, adrenaline coursing through me.

There's... there's so much... blood.

"Digi! Digi...oh please, no!"

I look, and Dillon's looming over me now. "What the fuck is wrong with you? He's just a kid! He's my brother!"

Just then Digi coughs up blood before his glossed over eyes look at me. All I see is fear, utter fear, like he's terrified of dying and it scares me how close he might be to it. I try my damndest not to show it. His hand reaches for mine and I take it, kissing his knuckles and praying he'll live out his young life and not die here because of me.

"Just hold on Digi, we'll get you help, okay? Don't talk." His hand covers where the bullet entered.

This is all my fault.

I look to see where the damage is, and luckily, it's the lower part of his left abdomen. His spleen might be the only major organ affected, but without a medical degree, I can't be too sure. I grab a towel from the counter and press it against the wound.

"Ahhhhh!!!"

"Will you shut him up?!" Dillon barks, but I ignore him.

"I'm sorry, Digi, but we have to keep pressure on it. Just hold it there and don't move, okay?" I spin around to confront Dillon. "You son of a bitch! Call an ambulance or he could die!"

I became enraged, beating his chest and screaming hysterically until he flung me to the ground.

He was enraged, his face contorted with fury, and his eyes burned with a hateful light as he pointed the gun at me. "Don't you *ever* hit me again, you got it? I may not be so gentle next time. We're not calling an ambulance. One of the guys coming can treat his wound. Or he could die for all I care. He wasn't part of the plan, anyway. Then again, neither was the neanderthal but I'll chalk that up to luck."

"What do you want? Why are you doing this?!"

Seeing my two guys lying there, I cry out in anguish, the raw pain of my emotions nearly unbearable.

Dillon sits on the sofa looking at the developing scene, "Well, you see... your little biker boy toy is worth more than he knows, and he's got a date with a very dangerous man. Once I get him there, I couldn't care less. I take my money and go. No need to continue to be a lawyer's lackey. I'm going to take my money and be in Tahiti fucking the first pairs of legs I can open.

It's disappointing that you're spoken for. I would've loved having you in the sack. You look like a screamer, possibly a biter?" The upper inflection indicated he was asking but also assuming. He growls, winking at me, and I feel physically sick.

"What do you mean I was promised?" He leans back while checking his phone and chuckles.

"Yes, my client has taken a liking to you, so he staked his claim. You're going to be his prized whore and there's nothing you can do to stop it." His laugh is deep and sinister. It didn't register, there was too much going on.

Suddenly, there's a knock that caused me to jump. He stands up and walks towards the door.

"Oh, and here comes the calvary. Too bad you won't get answers until you wake up. Sweet dreams, buttercup."

Before I could respond, he pulls and shoots the dart gun, or at least I hoped it was. A fiery burn hits my shoulder and spreads as I fade to black...

Johnny

"Fucking hell Dillon, what happened here?! All you had to do was get her to the compound."

Johnny looks at the entire situation before him. It looked like a crime scene with three bodies on the floor.

"How the hell was I supposed to know he'd come to see her. We were on the date and all I had to do was wine and dine her, then get her back here to tranquilize her. The little bastard got in the way, but we also nabbed him, too. It's a win-win. Glad you gave me a tranquilizer gun. He's fucking huge. He could have pummeled me. Now order your lackeys to get them in the car or van or whatever you brought. I did you a goddamned favor, you fucking ingrate."

Cupid

I'm surrounded by darkness; I don't remember what happened before I tried to tell her... something... what the hell was it? I know it was important, and it was on the tip of my tongue before the... burning? I feel like I'm floating in an empty abyss.

I hope I'm not dead. I can't be. There's no white light unless I'm in purgatory. I didn't think I did anything that bad to warrant that, but I'm stuck wherever I am.

I need to make it right; I need to make US right. I need to tell her I love her. That's what it was... I love her!

A wave of warmth spreads through me as I declare it, a feeling of perfect alignment.Being in love feels like coming home, a perfect fit. Being in love feels right. I have to get back to her.

Johnny

"Mr. Wellington, sir?" Johnny knocks lightly, then slides in the door, looking at the back of the desk chair, awaiting a response.

"Johnny, you better have some good news. I'm tired of your failure." Johnny walks further into his office and stands next to the seat in front of the desk.

"Actually, it's great news. Dillon got the girl and your son. They're in the warehouse, but there was a slight hiccup... with one of his club members there, just a dumb kid. He needs medical attention."

Mr. Wellington stands from his desk, fixing his expensive suit, and looks at him. "Just patch him up. Even if he survives, we'll put a bullet in his head. Speaking of bullets, don't forget to get rid of that slimy lawyer. He won't see his payout. Let's get this going. It's time for me to see...my son."

Cupid

"Fuck! Owww... where the hell am I?"

A throbbing pain hammers behind my eyes, a dull pulse matching the frantic beat in my temples. Each blink is a slow, agonizing effort, the world swimming in blurry color. My head weighs a ton, a leaden pressure resisting every attempt to lift it. Slowly, the hazy edges sharpen, revealing a clearer, though still unsteady, view. I realize I'm bound to a chair when I make out the ropes around my abdomen, arms, and legs.

I try once more to lift my head, my eyes squinting, and feel the dull throb behind my temples. I see her... lying on the ground, she's not moving. Her dress is raised a bit and her shoes are gone. Her arm covers her face. I can't see if she's breathing or hurt.

"Lyr-lyric, baby, can you hear me? Sweetheart, say something." My throat is so dry, like I'm gargling hot Saharan sand. It hurts to talk, but I have to know. She's not moving. I need to get to her; I don't know if she's alive or...

She moved! Her slight movement reassured me she was still present. Thank god, I think she heard me... hold on kitten, I'm coming for you.

A door swings open. "Look who's finally awake. Well, hello lover boy, rise and shine!"

I know that smug, arrogant voice. The rage builds as I hear his sinister laugh. I see his expensive shoes in front of me and then he crouches down. A pathetic junkie in an expensive suit. And there he was, the man I wanted dead the most, Johnny fucking Picardio.

"Hey sunshine, nice of you to wake just in time. How's the head feeling? I gave Dillon some highly concentrated tranquilizers. I'm glad too, I didn't need you rearranging anyone's face, especially mine. You've done enough damage there. But there's no problem there now, is it?!"

The repeated slaps sting, the last one a jarring blow that violently yanks my head and leaves me trembling and fighting to free myself from the chair.

"Now, now, you're not getting out just yet. You have an important meeting to attend with my boss. Don't worry, I'll keep an eye out on your sweet little thing."

"You touch her I'll rip you in fucking half. You threatened to rape her, you sick son of a bitch!"

"Well, it's not me you have to worry about. My boss has claimed her and I don't have any say in what he does with her, and neither do you." He chuckles as he walks back out.

As soon as he's gone, I call out to her again. No answer, but then I hear groaning behind me.

I try to turn my head, but I can't.

Someone else is here.

"Ughhhhh... what the hell?"

I hear shuffling. Maybe they're free and can at least get to her to see if she's okay. "Who's that, who's there?"

"Cu-cupid?"

"Digi? Is that you? What are you doing here?"

He groans, he sounds like he's in pain. "I-I came out of the bedroom after I heard a loud thunk and he shot me."

"Shot you where?! Can you move? How bad is it?"

I'm going to kill that motherfucker, so help me.

His breathing is shallow, I can tell. "My lower stomach. It hurts like a bitch, but I'm okay. Where's Lyric? I'm tied to a post; I can't see her or you."

"I see her. She's in front of me, but she hasn't moved. Do you know if they shot her?"

"I-I don't think so. I blacked out right after I heard the shot, then I woke up tied up. What do they want?"

Good question that I didn't have an answer for.

"I don't know, but we need to get her conscious. They never tied her up."

I see a cloud of dust coming from her head as she coughs. "Lyric, can you hear me? Lyric!"

Then the door opens again. First, that bastard Johnny walks in with a Cheshire grin, then as he moves out of the way, someone else walks in. As soon as our eyes met, I recognized the man behind him... the tall, well-dressed gentleman, who walked in with utter confidence. He was the direction of all my rage.

Black Aces

"Hey, has anyone heard from Digi or seen Cupid since his ride to "get some fresh air?"

Blondie holds up his hand in air quotes.

Everyone shook their heads. Club stands up from his seat and signals everyone to follow him. He goes to Digi's room. It's a typical room turned pigsty.

Club wades through the room straight to his computer. "He told me he has a tracking chip embedded in the emblem of his cut. He said we all do because he... he was afraid to lose someone. Kid's a freaking genius, I tell you."

His face falls a bit as he tries to shake the thought while he boots up his computer.

He goes to a red "X" icon and Jackal leans forward. "Crossfind?"

"Yeah, it's the program he uses to keep tabs on us. See, these red dots are us in the house, but if we pan out, we should be able to locate them."

"Pan out to the hotel. They couldn't have gone too far.

Maybe they're with Lyric, and he's finally telling her how he feels."

He zooms out toward the downtown area where the hotel is. "Nothing. I'm going to pan out further. Somebody call them to see if they pick up. No, wait! He told me he put a chip in Lyric's phone when she was bunking with him and they had grown close. Besides, she didn't wear a cut. Call her cell. Maybe we can get coordinates to where they are."

Cheetah pulls his phone out and dials. "She's not picking up." He whispers.

"Don't hang up. I can use it to find her signal."

Her voicemail picks up, and he leaves a calm message like nothing was wrong so that it could stay connected longer.

"Hey Lyric, it's Cheetah but I'm sure you saw the caller ID... We, uh...we miss having you around. Let us know when you get back to the hotel and are free. We want to take you out to dinner. Give one of us a ring or call the house number, okay?"

He hangs up and Blondie screeches. "Genius Cheetah, that gave me enough time to track her down. Looks like... uh, they are about 40 miles west of here, at someplace out in the middle of nowhere. I got a bad feeling about this."

Jackal nods, "I agree and look, when you zoom to that area, there's the other two signals, they're all together. Okay everybody, strap up it's going to be a long ride and we need to be prepared for any and everything. They may be okay, or they may be in grave danger. Let's not risk it. We need to bring our family home."

Everyone strap up for the long ride...to the middle of nowhere.

Unknown

"Mr. Wellington? What... what the fuck are you doing here? What do you want with me or her or my brother? I don't understand..."

"Patience, lad, I'll explain everything to you in due time. Johnny, make sure the little filly is still breathing."

I notice how irate he is with my request, and I hold my hand up to stop Johnny. "Never mind. Bobby, make sure she's okay. She *is* precious cargo. Johnny, go busy yourself somewhere. Your presence is pissing off my guest."

"Who gives a fuck about what I do to his feelings! He's the bane to my goddamn existence and I would like nothing more than to put a bullet between his eyes." He pulls his gun out, rushes towards him and presses his ivory inlay silver 9mm to his forehead.

I snap my fingers and two of my men disarm and pull Johnny back to me.

"Hey! You listen to what the fuck I say! I need him alive for now. Now go take a goddamn walk... NOW!"

Johnny storms out, busting through the doors.

I turn back to Aleister. "Apologies for that little outburst. I bet you're wondering what all this has to do with you? Well, you see, the situation is far more complicated than you think."

"Stop beating around. I don't have time for this! Just tell me what this is!"

I chuckle. "I think you have more than enough time. You're not going anywhere, anytime soon. But her... she'll be leaving with me and become something very useful to me. I heard you had a taste of her... should have locked that in, but no matter, she belongs to me now."

"Over my dead body!"

I snap my fingers. "Exactly! I'm glad you're finally seeing things my way. You see, I'll put a bullet in your head and your buddy there and hop on my private jet to head back to L.A. with that delicious piece of ass. I can't wait to make that little vixen my personal fleshlight. Your mom was a screamer. She loved it when I was rough with her. It gave her the most intense orgasms. Any who, I suppose I still owe you an explanation about your mother, huh?"

Cupid

It's infuriating that he left my mother heartbroken and destroyed, and then has the audacity to team up with the man who finished her off. I don't know who I want dead more.

"Why her, huh? All my mom wanted was your affection! If you couldn't give her that, why even start a relationship with her?"

He paces in front of me, his expensive alligator shoes scraping against the floor, which made me realize my Lyric is lying on the cold ground. This New Mexico heat means that warehouses like this are equipped with powerful air conditioners, particularly for products that the heat could damage. I may not be cold, or at least not as cold as she would be lying on the floor

Mr. Wellington lights a Cohiba cigar, puffing away like he was celebrating. "There's a lot you didn't know about my relationship with your mother. We met way before you met me, over 30 years ago. I was just starting at my father's business, a multimillion-dollar firm. I had it all by association, money, power, women, and sex. I had more pussy than I knew what to do with! I wasn't looking to settle down, not when I had my pick of a fresh piece of ass every night. No way! But my dad didn't like my reputation as a playboy. He knew where to hit me, where it hurts...my pockets and my inheritance. That's when daddy dearest made a life-changing decision..." He walks and stands over Lyric, then squats down.

"Get away from her! Don't you touch her!"

He smirks while standing back up and nudges her with his shoe. She groans and moves a fraction, shaking from the cold ground. I had to swallow my pride.

"Please. She's cold. At least put her on a blanket or something to keep her warm. I'm begging you."

He eyes me, then her and huffs, snapping his fingers. "Get a blanket, put her on it." The man leaves and comes back with a blanket that looks thick enough to combat the chill. They move her, but she's still listless. They lay her on top and wrap the rest over her.

"Looks like I found your Achilles' heel. I can see why, though. I had a brief run-in with her when she was at her bar cleaning the countertop. I mean wow. She was soaking wet in her white tee and red bra, like a bikini carwash babe. I would have fucked her then, but I was there on business. I had to make sure the Ramirez family received their shipment. They're known for various methods of castration. There's nothing I value more than my dick. Anyway, back to your mother."

He sets a chair in front of me. "My father changed his will to stipulate that his money would go to his first-born grandchild, not his son. Crazy, right? I mean, why was I being punished for living my life and being a ladies' man?

Well, I wasn't going to let him win. No way, that money rightfully belongs to me!"

He snapped his fingers, and someone placed an expensive glass of scotch in his hand. Judging by his suit and his demeanor, it was expensive. I could smell the premium quality.

"Want one? Oh, guess not since you can't hold it, but let me tell you, it's rather good. Imported from Belize. Where was I? Oh yeah, daddy's little surprise. But I devised a plan. I had a drug run from Mexico to Vegas with a stop in New Mexico. I met a pretty little lady there who seemed easy enough to convince that I was her Romeo coming to save her. Didn't take much, though. She was pathetically desperate for attention and that intimate touch. I told her what she wanted to hear, you know, that she was beautiful, she was special, blah, blah, blah... and I had her that night. Man, she was a screamer!"

I cringe as he chuckles, taking another sip. I noticed Lyric move a little out of the corner of my eye. I hope she doesn't wake in the middle of this nightmare.

Lyric

I'm conscious, finally. After being moved from the cold floor to a blanket, I remain relatively still. I move just a little because I know he's worried. I make small, deliberate movements looking for my phone. I put it in my bra before my 'date' with that backstabbing bastard.

I feel the numbers trying to dial the clubhouse from memory. I push the volume button until it's as low as possible. I hear it ring... and ring... and ring. I don't hang up; I need somebody to pick up.

Someone is talking to Cupid; I'm not paying attention to the conversation I need to hear when someone picks up the phone. I wonder where Digi is, too? They shot him, and I just hope he wasn't...

No, I have to think positive. He's okay. He's okay.

I bring the phone closer to my ear and groan to make them think I was still unconscious.

Then it clicks over. I hear wind and... engine noises?

"Black Aces, this is Jackal."

"Jackal, help!" I whisper yell enough for him to hear me, but not them inside the room.

"Lyric, sweetie. Don't worry, we're coming for you. We're tracking your phone. Don't do anything. Stay safe, we're coming."

"Okay."

I clutch the phone after hearing him hang up, praying for my life, my brother's life, and the man who holds my heart. I hope he can keep his temper at bay because I can hear raised voices. Who knows how dangerous this man is. The question really was, *who was he?*

Cupid

He takes another long sip. "Anyway, I knew it doesn't always work after the first fuck, so I carried on a 'relationship' with her, filling her up as many times as I could while feeding her the American dream. I even took her to L.A. to show daddy that I had settled down and he fell for it. He created an account here in her name, so the money had somewhere to deposit. Until the kid was 18, she was the executor to the account."

My head was spinning as I was gathering his info to what

my mom told me. I remember when she gave me access to an account, at 18, that had eight grand in it, saying she was saving for me to be on my own.

If what he says is true... then that would make him...

"You're...my father."

A sinister smile forms. "Hello, son."

A searing inferno consumes me, a furious rage erupting from the deepest, darkest caverns of my being. My body trembles violently, each shudder a physical manifestation of the anger within.

"Yeah, I didn't think you'd take the news well, which is why you're still tied, but it doesn't matter. You'll be dead soon. No retribution for mommy."

I close my eyes to summon my darkness. Even the demons would fear my rage towards my...*father.*

"Oh, and before you try to negotiate, I will put a bullet in her head if you do not accept your fate. All whores are the same, but this sweet little treat will be one of my prized possessions."

His laugh was sinister, maniacal. My hatred for the pathetic man before me numbed all the pain I'd felt.

Up close, the resemblance is striking. His thin lips, mirroring my own Cupid's bow, curve into a faint smile. I see the tiny cleft in his chin, a familiar imperfection I used to prod as a child, now hidden by my beard. Even the same deep-set, shadowed eyes stare back; a puzzle solved, seems the demon seed had stronger genes.

My father... I was looking into the eyes of my father.

"Ahh, now it has sunk in, can you see the similarities now? In another lifetime, we could have been the perfect father and son, but fate dealt you a cruel hand. Living in squalor with a very unstable mother who..."

"You made her that way! Don't you fucking talk about her like she was crazy! You're the psychopath that used and abused her, discarded her like she was nothing and for what, money? She wasn't nothing, she was my everything, she was my mother!"

I'm so pissed I can't even cry. I want to get away from here and take my precious kitten with me, but I don't think I'll make it out of this. I have to make peace with the fact that I will probably die here. But it'll be worth it if she and Digi make it out alive. She could take him and live on the beach like she always dreamed and I would watch from the heavens and be at peace knowing she was safe. If only I had gotten the balls to tell her how much I love her.

Lyric

I tossed and turned, facing Aleister and the mysterious man I'd heard was his father! I peeked open one eye to see my love bound to a chair, furious and heartbroken as the man insulted his mother.

It's too much for him to bear. The weight of it all, a crushing pressure on his chest made him stare, eyes fixed on a ghost of his past. The man who abandoned his mother, the man...wait, he was that older man who walked in my bar!

Now I remember how he eyed me down when I was soaked in water, how he licked his lips and stared at my bra and his subtle flirt when he said he'd return and buy me a drink. Oh my god, it was his dad!

I try to listen in. "All whores are the same, but this little sweet treat will be one of my prized possessions."

Wait, is he talking about me? I'm not going anywhere with that bastard! I rotate, keeping one eye open and the other closed so no one will notice. His guards are pea-brained morons as they leave to take a smoke break, leaving their boss by himself. I hope Jackal and the guys get here soon!

In the meantime, maybe I could sneak up and knock him out!

With what, Lyric? Your nifty cellphone?

I peek again and see that he has a gun in his holster and Aleister's screaming about how he hurt his mother. I notice movement on a metal beam behind him. There are hands tied with a rope and they are shifting side to side and that's when I notice the outline of the club's emblem on their back.

Digi! He's still alive, but I know he's hurt and desperately needs medical attention. I can't lie here; I need to see if he's okay. At least I can help him if I can't help Aleister.

I had to decide. Stay, and lie in wait or help my little brother?

Cupid

Look, I'm not here to be berated by you about your mother. I'm here for my inheritance, Dad's millions, not yours. Your thirtieth birthday is in four hours; then the $35 million hits your account, thanks to Grandpa. I'll get rid of you, play the grieving father routine, and claim the money. These small town banks are easy to manipulate; I'll give them the performance of a lifetime! So, let's enjoy these last few hours as father and son."

I couldn't help but laugh at the notion, "So, I would have what? Walk into the bank one day and discover there's an extra 35 mil in there and what, you think I'd be excited to be an instant millionaire? Money means nothing to me. I'm nothing like you. I don't care about wealth. How fucking shallow can you be? I have everything in my club, brotherhood and a place to belong, people who have my back!"

He stands by her still body. "And what about her? Do you care for her, like you do your boys, or is she just something to get you off at night?"

I inhale deeply and sigh out my frustration at his harsh words. She was much more than just a lay. I stared at her and her beautiful hair, smooth but dirty skin, and knowing how deeply she cared for me, my answer was clear.

"No... I love her. She's my world and I wish I had told her sooner."

"Aww, sounds like remorse. I don't care for love or anything. You obviously got that weakness from your mother." He scoffs as he walks back to the bar cart to fix another drink.

I realized then that I *was* like my love struck mother but tried to cover it by being like him, cold and heartless, but I wasn't him and being in love wasn't weak.

Lyric

My heart fluttered wildly. I heard it with my own ears. He loves me! Aleister said that he loved me! He finally said those words I've been waiting to hear, but in the worst situation. I can't act like a corpse anymore. I make slight movements and groan before I sit up holding my head, squinting, before seeing him.

"Ugh, Aleister? Where am I?" Looking over, I could see how relieved he was.

"Lyric, baby, are you okay?"

I groan at the stiffness of my neck and body, "I think so.

Did you... did you mean what you said?" I felt the tears well up.

He nodded, "Absolutely kitten, I love you so much. I knew the very moment we shared our first kiss. It's always been you. I'm sorry I kept you waiting. I was scared."

I couldn't help but laugh while crying, "I love you too, baby. It's okay, I understand. I never wanted to rush you." I forgot my surroundings and sat up to run over and hug him until I was looking down the barrel of a gun and I stumbled back.

"Ah ah ahhh... albeit a sweet gesture. Let's remember why we're all here. As soon as the money hits your account, I can put a bullet in your head and take the money and your girl."

Is he serious?

"What, what do you want with me?!"

"Oh, since I saw your delicious tits soaking wet at the bar, I knew I had to have you and soon money will be no object. We could fly anywhere in the world. You could have an orgasm in a different country every single day."

I scoot away from him. "Get away from me! I love your son. I'd rather die with him than be anywhere near you!"

He cocks the gun and I gasp, suddenly frozen in fear. "Don't fucking tempt me, Princess. You're as useful as he is. I was giving you the chance to bang the original. Come on baby, why don't you try daddy? I bet you my dick is much bigger than my son's and I've been told I'm an amazing lover."

I physically gag. "Ugh, hard pass. Do you realize that you have us hostage so that you can kill your own son for money. You're despicable!" I huffed.

His dad scoffed as he waved in Aleister's direction. "Whatever, I didn't want no kid! I wanted that money and I was going to do anything to get it and I did." He gripped the back of my neck really tight, causing me to reach back, trying to loosen it. His grin was pure evil.

"Wait, why are we still talking about this?! I will put a bullet in his head and yours too, Princess, if you don't shut up and come with me. Don't forget the kid, he's real expendable. Are you willing to let him die?"

"You let him go. He's just a kid!"

He laughs, glancing at Digi. "Well, sucks for you, kid. This is a *fatal* lesson in bad timing." Then he turns back to me, "Maybe if you agree to come with me, I'll spare him."

Oh god, I want to projectile vomit at his vile comments. He pulls me roughly by my hair, but I wouldn't give him the satisfaction of hearing me cry out in pain. I grit my teeth, breathing roughly.

"Now, what's it going to be? Come and be my slut so I can fuck you unconscious and the boy lives."

I had no choice. I didn't want to, but Digi was as close to me as my biological brothers and I would do anything for him. I saw the heartbreak on Cupid's face. He wanted to help me. He wanted to save me, but he couldn't.

I swallow my pride. "Okay. Just promise to free him and... I'll go."

If you could see how shocked Aleister was that I agreed to go with his dad. "Lyric, don't! He'll kill Digi once you get on the jet!"

I try to walk towards him, but he yanks me back. "No way. You can say what you have to say right here." He runs his hands down my side, brushing my breast and I shudder violently. The tears fall and I can't stop them if I try.

"Baby... I can't let Digi die. He's innocent in all this. My life doesn't matter but his, it's just starting. I-I love you...so much and I'll always remember that as the best moment of our...last night together."

He's trying to hold back the tears. "Don't give up on me, please! I need you..." Words never sounded sweeter than those words right there.

Simultaneously, I felt the gun shoved into my side and saw the flash and felt a burning, aggravating sensation in my side, growing outward from where the pain started before I looked down to my hand, instinctively clutching the fresh wound. Is that... blood? I looked at him and muttered out, "Aleister?"

A comforting void descended as the world faded to black. Well, everything *here* was okay...

Black Aces

Jackal and the gang park their bikes down the road from a compound that looked more like a factory than a residence, but there was a lavish mansion on the grounds.

Jackal gathers them to huddle. "Cheetah, are they still there?" He checks the app on his phone.

"Yeah, they are in that warehouse by the house."

Jackal then points at the compound. "We're going to split up. I need Cheetah with his speed and expertise with me. We will head to the warehouse and take out whatever threat is there. The rest will storm the house. This is a bloodbath. Our brothers are in there with Cupid's girl. We don't even know if they are alive, but we will not leave without them. We will not take hostages, it is kill or be killed. I try not to condone this extreme type of violence, but there are exceptions to the rules. This has been boiling over, and now it is at the tipping point. Is everyone clear?"

Slipping through the gate, they crept past two men in guard uniforms. Knox swiftly slit one's throat while Club snapped the other's neck. They collapsed, their bodies discarded near the building to conceal them from view.

Knox and Club head around to the back of the house while Blondie goes through the front door.

Despite its desert location, the house was impeccably clean, a stark contrast to the surrounding arid landscape; not a speck of sand was in sight. Blondie looked around and noted both floors, but no one was around. He headed straight back to the kitchen.

Knox and Club took out three more men who appeared to be on a cigarette break. To save on ammunition, they stabbed two and by the time the third reached for his gun, Club had already pulled his .45 caliber and fired the kill shot right between his eyes, then confiscated his weapon.

Cheetah had taught everyone to shoot comfortably and with practice, Club was easily second-best behind him.

They leave their bodies where they are, not caring about being found now. They needed to find their brothers and their sister.

Cupid

"LYRIC!" Digi screamed. I'm not sure if he saw anything from his position, but he knew. There's no mistaking the sound of a gunshot. I hear pain fill his voice.

"Cupid! Cupid, what happened? Is she okay? Please! Say something!"

Panic seized him as I numbly watched her collapse, a small pool of blood welling between her fingers.

"You shot her, you son of a bitch! Why?! She's all I had!"

He nudges her body, and she falls to the side, motionless. Her hand is still clutching the wound.

"Look what you made me do! I wanted to take her in more ways than one, but it was obvious she was stuck on my son...my useless, pathetic, worthless son! Now you and her can meet in the great beyond, happily ever after or whatever."

My love was dying before my eyes, and I felt numb. Her last words, a cherished memory of our time together, echoed in my ears.

God, I wish we had more time.

That bastard shot her like she was nobody. How was I supposed to go on without her? How do I break the news to Digi? I could hear him crying because I didn't answer, and he assumed. I wish he wasn't right.

It didn't matter anymore. He could have the money; I didn't care if I died in an hour. My life was meaningless. My heart shattered again, beyond repair.

Fuck life. It wasn't worth living without her. I felt my entire being give up and my head slumped down.

"Now, now, son, let's not be down. You'll be together soon enough. There's only...35 minutes left."

I was sick of hearing his fucking voice.

"Why don't you just shoot me now? What does it matter when I die?"

"Because there will be an autopsy, and it needs to say you died on your birthday, not beforehand. If not, then the money goes to an anonymous charity. It's all in the details of the will."

He sits in the chair in front of me, tapping the butt of the gun against the metal chair. I let the tears fall. I was so enraged, so heartbroken. I couldn't even look at him.

At least she would finally meet my mom, the other love of my life.

Black Aces

Jackal radioed Club for a status. He confirmed they had cleared the house and killed ten guys just low-level cronies. No one of real importance, leading him to believe that all the higher-ups, whoever they are, must be in the warehouse. They continue to sweep the house as Cheetah and Jackal reach the metal structure. There are minimal windows, but they peep in to see Johnny at his desk, snorting a line, waiting for the effects to take place.

Then, a girl walks in.

It's that bitch, Trixie.

Nothing shocked them. A woman as vile as that would hang around her own kind.

Jackal has never been a fan of club bunnies, but he knew his guys were young and horny, so he allowed them. In the back of his mind, he always knew she was trouble from day one. Her obsession with Cupid was obvious.

He focuses back on the commotion inside as Trixie bends over Johnny's desk, shoving her tits up.

"Johnny, come on... fuck me. I need to feel that dick so deep inside of me." Her nasally whine is like nails on a chalkboard. Jackal thought to himself, he'd never get hard listening to that, probably why Johnny uses drugs.

Johnny shakes his head, lights a cigarette, then he unzips his pants and whips it out.

"Take care of me first and maybe I'll fuck you. Get on your knees, slut."

She disrobes quickly and plops down in front of him and goes to work.

Jackal finds a way inside that brings him straight to Johnny's wide-open door. He stands off to the side.

"Fuck baby girl, deep throat it, that's it. Don't forget my balls, too. Yeah, like that. Such a filthy slut. You'll fuck anyone for a hit, huh?"

Johnny pushes her head further and further down his shaft until she's flushed against him, struggling to breathe. She smacks his hands so she can come up for air.

Inhale

"Asshole! Are you trying to suffocate me?!" He shrugs as she gets some deep breaths before diving back in. It doesn't take long before he's holding her head still as he grunts. "Oh, I'm... coming... ugh! That's a good girl. Now hop on this dick and ride me."

She licks her lips and straddles him, sliding down. "Ooh... yes, daddy."

They are going at it, giving Cheetah enough time to sneak through the warehouse and position himself on the other side of the door just as she was about to reach her climax. Or he hoped she was. She was as shrill as a blow horn.

"Joh-Johnny, fuck! I'm coming, baby. Oh god!"

She screams and Cheetah winces before drawing his gun.

"Alright, get the fuck off me, sheesh!" But she was panting from their wild session, holding on to him.

Cheetah waited for the lovers to finish before stepping through the door. Johnny noticed Cheetah and quickly went to grab his gun. He stood up, causing her to drop to the floor. His penis was flaccid from their activity, but glistened in her orgasm. Before he could raise his gun, Cheetah fired twice, shattering his kneecaps. Trixie screamed, but Cheetah shut her up by winging her in the shoulder. Actually, it didn't shut her up, but rendered her useless.

As Johnny screamed and convulsed on the floor, Jackal calmly walked into the office. "You son of a bitch! I'll have you all killed! That boy and his bitch, too!"

Jackal towers over him and laughs. "Big threats coming from a fucking lackey. All your men are dead, Johnny, and you're lucky you aren't. No, I'm leaving you for Cupid. I'm sure he has some ideas on how to make you suffer. And you,"

He turns to the sniveling whore on the ground.

"The cops came by to tell Lyric it was *you* who set her place on fire. You left evidence all over. It doesn't take much to know an overused jealous slut set the place on fire. Were you upset because Lyric is Cupid's ol' lady, and not you?"

She stares daggers at him with fire in her eyes. "Fuck you! She's temporary. Nobody can keep him satisfied like I can! I'll kill her before I let them be together!" Cheetah places the barrel between her eyes, and she gasps loudly. "Or how about I put a bullet between your whore eyes and discard you in the desert for the coyotes to pick at your heavily used body? If I see you anywhere near our town, I'll have no trouble finishing the job. *No one* will miss you."

That shut her up. Usually, Jackal doesn't condone violence towards women, but she was no woman, a useless sperm dumpster, and that was being generous. But still...

Jackal pushes Cheetah's arm with the gun down and shakes his head. "Cheetah, no. We need to find everyone."

Johnny laughs sinisterly, "It's almost midnight and the second it is, he'll be dead by the hands of his father!"

His father?

Cupid mentioned he didn't know who he was and didn't care to know. Jackal was confused. Why was his father here, and why was he trying to kill his own flesh and blood? He quickly checks his watch, 11:55 pm.

"We got to go; they're not going anywhere. And if you try, Cheetah will put a bullet in your head so fast you won't even know you're in hell until it's too late. Come on!" They close the door while Johnny yells obscenities at them, but no one fucking cared.

They needed to save their family.

Cupid

"11:58 pm, almost killing time. Any last words, son?" His words, like icy shards, echoed in my brain, accompanied by a rasping, chilling laugh that scraped against my eardrums. The bitter taste of defiance rose in my throat; I would no longer repress the storm brewing within.

"You motherfucker! I can't believe you did this! Why didn't you just ask for the money? I want nothing to do with you or my grandfather. Not knowing you was a blessing, and you threw it all away. Go ahead, kill me. I've got nothing left. My life's meaningless without her." My gaze falls upon her lifeless form. Each time I say I'm dead inside, it feels true. I'm ready to die...to be with my love and mother. The clock chimed, and the last bit of rage poured out of me. "Do it! You sick son of a bitch! You took everything from me! I hope you choke on it and live a miserable life!"

He points the gun, cocks it, and sighs. Hmmm... well, happy 30th birthday, son..."

I close my eyes, dreaming of the moment I'll be with both my girls again.

Bang

"Ugh!"

Lyric

It's so cold. Am I dead? He shot me; I must be dead. I never got to spend my life with Aleister, never got to feel his hand on my cheeks so I can stare at him lovingly when he tells me he loves me. Never got to walk out to the beach from our house and enjoy the breeze as we walk along the shore. Aleister would squeeze my hand so I would pay attention. He would stop me and kiss me gently; my entire body would be on fire. I miss him, the way he kissed me, the way he touched me, the way he made love to me. I needed him like my next breath.

Inhales sharply

Wait, I'm breathing... I'm alive? I'm alive! It hurts to move; it hurts to breathe. That bastard shot me! I can't hear well or see anything, it's like a wavering tone in my ear. It sounds like a hundred muffled voices all at once.

Someone pulls my body and lays me on my back. Something waves in front of me rapidly and I can vaguely hear what sounds like my name.

Someone's calling my name!

I got to snap out of this. I want to go home! I want to be home with my family! I tried to squeak or elicit a sound from my throat, but all I could do was cough. "That's it Lyric, come back to us. Come back to your family..."

Cupid

An icy dread grips me as I wait for the bullet, its trajectory a swift end to this life, piercing my heart, head, neck, or any vital point. The silence screams louder than any gunshot.

But nothing happens. There's no sharp jab, excruciating pain, or white light before I see heaven's gate.

I open my eyes and look down to see blood splatter all over me... but it isn't mine. I don't think. My eyes focus finally, and I see Cheetah putting his pistol back in the holster and I see my father writhing on the ground from a gunshot wound...to his stomach?

Cheetah never misses. Why didn't he kill him?

Jackal walks over and looks at me while trying to cut the ropes. He's murmuring something, but I can't focus very well.

He frees me and pulls me up to stand. "You got to focus Cupid, come on, come back!" He smacks me a few times, but I'm still shocked and heartbroken. I'm standing, I'm alive, but I'm comatose.

My head turns slowly as I watch Club behind me untie

Digi, who immediately runs to Lyric lying on the floor. My kitten, she didn't deserve this. All she wanted was my love and all I want now was to give it to her, but she's gone.

Oh God, I lost her! All my thoughts revolve around her, what was, and what could have been. I'm a lost soul, cursed to walk this Earth alone.

"She's... and the... is on... way! ... you...me? Lyric... alive, snap out..."

I only understood bits and pieces of what he was saying until I felt my body jerk forward into the present and I was back.

"Huh, what..." He turned my body to see that they placed her on the blanket. Digi applied pressure to the wound despite his own gunshot wound. It looked like the bleeding had stopped. No doubt he had been holding it with his hand the entire time. He was squeezing her hand, trying to get her to open her eyes and respond. Her chest was barely rising and falling, but she was breathing!

As I tried to get my legs working, I felt something tugging on my pant leg and looked down to see my pathetic father.

"Help me, son, help...help your father! We can make it right, we can heal from this, just help me!"

Isn't this a fucking hallmark moment? Is he kidding?

I must be delusional to hear those words spewing from his mouth. Jackal pats my back to get me away from him, but in that moment of everything he put me through, I steal his pistol from behind his back and empty two rounds into my father's balls without flinching.

Those ear-piercing screams give me a strange sense of satisfaction.

"Guess you won't be fucking anymore, but I hope you get thoroughly fucked in jail. Fuck you...*dad.*"

I hand the gun back to Jackal as I try to get closer to her. I drop to my knees and bend down. Club moves out of the way, opposite of Digi. I take her hand and watch her chest rise and fall.

"I'm sorry kitten, I should have told you sooner. I love you so much. Please don't die. I need you. We all do. I want to grow old with you anywhere you want to go. Just please, come back to us." I squeeze her hand as the sirens get louder and louder, praying for a miracle.

The paramedics get there and put her on a stretcher.

"White female, age unknown, penetrating trauma from GSW to the side, heavy bleeding and possible hemorrhaging. No exit wound, breathing shallow and connected to oxygen, status critical. We need to get her back urgently. Are any of you family and can come with us now?"

All the words were swirling around, and I could barely comprehend.

"We all are, but her husband needs to go." Jackal shoves me forward. The paramedic tells me to follow them, and I do. I look back and another set of medics are prepping Digi for transport with Club accompanying him. Jackal, Knox, and Blondie are with the cops explaining the situation.

"Cupid, go!" Jackal's voice rang loud as I followed behind the gurney. One paramedic hops up front to start the trek to the hospital. We were in the middle of nowhere. Were we close to Van Hollen Medical, or did we have to go elsewhere? The other paramedic starts tending to her.

"Hurry Vincent, she's going to need a blood transfusion, or we'll lose her."

I shook at those very words. I couldn't lose her. I watched him move around the tiny space grabbing bags, bandages and sterilizing what he needed to patch her up as best he could.

I was in shock. I felt like all I could do was watch.

"Don't worry, I'm going to do all I can to save your wife." He hooks up an IV to her arm and checks her stats. Once he got her as stable as he could, he came over and tended to my superficial wounds. I didn't care about me, only my angel, whose blue lips finally started turning back to a normal shade.

I missed those soft lips on mine.

She still wasn't responsive, and it worried me. The medic almost seemed to know what I was thinking. "I put her in an almost coma-like state to ease her from the pain of the gunshot wound. I don't know what damage the bullet caused or is causing because there is no exit wound from what I can see. She'll most likely go right into emergency surgery and you'll have to wait. To be very blunt, she should be dead, but the mind can will itself to do anything and she wants to be here. She wants to be with you. She's one helluva fighter."

I couldn't help but smile at my little scrapper.

"I know."

We pull up to the emergency entrance and they whisk her away towards surgery. As I fill out the paperwork, my tears fall, and I pray to God to save the one person who makes my cold, dark life bearable. I needed her like my next breath.

While I wait, the police come and interrogate me about the events and I relay everything I could. I explained how they drugged and brought me there, how they kidnapped and shot her and Digi, my relationship with my dad, and the inheritance scam he was trying to pull.

I wanted him dead. I really wanted to do it myself, but I realized I would tear myself away from her had I done it. Besides, I found gratification in making that bastard a eunuch for the rest of his life. His dick might be gone, but his ass wasn't safe in prison.

Apparently, my assumptions were right as they found Trix and Johnny together, both shot. She confessed to burning the bar down in an act of jealousy and also admitted to gathering intel so that this entire plan could take place.

Paramedics brought Johnny to the hospital, handcuffed to the gurney. I saw them wheel him back to triage. Our eyes met momentarily, enough for him to mouth "Fuck you" before being carted off. I didn't give a shit about him or what happens to him now.

I hope the prison is handicap accessible.

Actually, no, I don't.

In the end, the police told me they would have to come back for her witness statement once she was well enough, and I agreed. The officer handed me his card just as my boys were coming in.

Jackal walks up and pulls me into a hug, a hug that radiated from a concerned parent, the fatherly hug I was always searching for. It was tight and filled with love and right now, I needed that.

I completely lost it, all my emotions of this terrible day/night streamed down my face. I fell to my knees, and he followed as I felt all my brothers surround me. I needed them just as much as when my mom died, if not more. My angel was fighting for her life, for our life together.

You wouldn't think that a group of burly, rugged men would show emotion like this, but as I said before, our club was different. We rode together and protected each other. Like a family, a family most of us never had. We didn't judge. We were all emotionally hurt or broken in one way or another. We knew, if anything, we had each other.

I couldn't sit still, and it was clear I needed to do something. Jackal gets my attention. "Hey, let's go visit Digi. I am sure he'd love to see his big brother." I had to see my little fighter, the bravest man I know.

We head down the hall, about five doors down, and there's a scrawny shirtless Digi watching television. Apparently, the bullet exited without major damage and he only needed to sterilize and staple the wound, his abdomen wrapped up tight to avoid infection.

Once he lays eyes on me, he instantly cries. I rush up and hug him, avoiding his bandages.

"I'm so sorry Digi, this is all my fault. You were right. I don't deserve her. You're a hero, you saved her."

He pulls back, shakes his head, and looks at me surprised, "What? No, I was just mad. I wanted you to see how much you DID need her. She needs you, too. I, I need you. Please, tell me, is she... she..." His lip quivered.

"No kiddo, she's still in surgery. There was no exit wound, and it definitely did some damage; we just have to wait. We have to be strong for her, okay?" I hug him tight. We stayed with him for about an hour watching some techie show about hacking into computer mainframes with just a cellphone and a ghost URL, whatever that meant. He was soaking in the information like a sponge and I was so confused, but he was happy and in his element. A glimpse of the old Digi, but I knew he wouldn't be quite the same.

There was a tap at the door and Club peeks in. "Hey Eros, the doctor wants to talk to you."

Digi squeezes my hand. "She's going to be okay; I can feel it. Tell her I miss her."

I made my way out the door and back down the hall where the doctor was waiting.

"Mr..." He waits for my response while holding out his hand. "McElroy, sorry doctor. Call me Aleister."

"Nice to meet you. I am Doctor Prentiss. I will be your wife's doctor for the duration of her stay. I'll be very honest with you. She sustained quite a bit of damage. The angle and velocity could have been deadly, but the bullet lodged itself in her rib, reducing further damage to any of her critical organs. We got in, removed the bullet, and stopped the bleeding."

I felt a huge weight off my shoulders. "Thank you, doctor."

"That's not all. With the damage, we did a full check from head to toe, you know, to make sure she didn't sustain brain damage or damage to her other major systems and... may I ask you a personal question?"

"I... uh yeah, sure." I trembled a little, fearing the worst, but then he smiled.

"Mr. McElroy, did you know your wife was pregnant?"

I heard several gasps behind me from my brothers. I was utterly speechless. I just shook my head.

"Well, let me assure you, the baby is fine. The bullet completely missed the amniotic sac. She's roughly six weeks along. Had she been further, she could have lost the baby. We have the baby on constant monitoring by a strap she's wearing around her abdomen. You'll get to see the baby's heartbeat on the monitor. We also added liquid prenatal meds to her drip to ensure the baby is getting the nutrients it needs while mommy is unconscious. Your wife will be in a medically induced coma for a few days while we track their healing process, okay? I assure you we are doing all we can for them."

I agree, and he squeezes my shoulder before walking away. I didn't move or make a sound; I was in shock.

Jackal steps in front of my line of sight with a big smile on his face.

"Did you hear that? My boy is about to be a father and me, a grandfather, and you all are uncles! Our first club baby, I think that's something we should all be thankful to come out of all this. Come on daddy, let's go see your girl." They all whoop and holler and congratulate me. I can feel the goosebumps forming as I realize...

I'm going to be a daddy.

Lyric

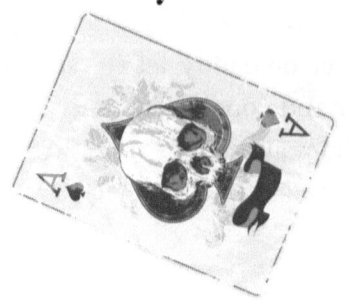

I really think I'm dead this time. The last thing I remember is Club or Knox talking to me, telling me to stay awake, but it hurt so much I felt myself slip into the soothing darkness.

Shit!

Wait... maybe I shouldn't be cursing if I am dead because then God probably heard me... yikes!

I can't die! I have so much to say and do and confess! My thoughts are all I have, and they weren't the best in my last moments. All the revelations from last night, this morning, or whatever day it is, made me feel like I was on a reality TV show.

No, really, what day is it?

I am brought out of my thoughts by a voice. It's all around me.

"Hey sweetheart, I'm here. You just focus on getting better and coming back to us. We love you, kitten. I love you."

It's Aleister! I scream his name, but it just echoes back. "Just a couple more days and the doctor said he'll bring you out of the coma. Can you hold on a few more days? I can't wait to see those beautiful eyes meet mine."

Coma? They shot me, so inducing a coma makes sense; I guess I have no choice, but I really miss him.

Cupid

It took a Herculean effort to convince me to go home. I'd been up for almost three days straight, barely eating a thing. Knox and Cheetah escorted me home, threatening to let Cheetah put a bullet in my ass if I didn't go to at least freshen up and take a nap. Knowing he wouldn't miss; I couldn't risk it.

The ride was long, but we got home in a little over an hour.

"Shower and change. I'll bring you something to eat before you lie down." Knox ordered; he was giving me no room to argue.

I open the door and stand against the doorframe, looking around. Eventually, I walk into my bathroom and turn on the shower, flashing back to the first time we had sex.

She felt amazing, inside and out. Her little pants and moans were music to my ears, the way she gazed at me lustfully and her falling apart in my arms. I shower, wash my hair, and trim my beard. I come out of the bathroom and head to my closet for something comfortable to wear. I chose some black sweats and a white t-shirt.

I lay face up on the bed and stare at the ceiling, thinking about her cuddled next to me in bed. Her smooth legs rubbing against mine, her tiny fingers tracing endlessly across my chest. Her stealthy grab of my beard.

I'm brought out of my thoughts by a knock and Knox

comes in with a tray of soup, a salad, and a sandwich. "I didn't know which to make, so I made them all. Eat up brother, or should I say daddy now? How are you taking the news?"

I sit up and inhale the delicious aroma. "I'm still in shock. I can't believe it. If it weren't for her, I would have never allowed myself to be happy. I would have dwelled in the past for the rest of my life."

"She's the spark that needed to be put in your life... we all saw it, day by day, she added and never asked for much, just you. Now you have everything you could ever need."

"And more..." Then my cell rang, and I didn't recognize the number. "Hello?"

"Mr. McElroy, this is Ben from First National Bank. I was calling to alert you to a sizable sum of money deposited into your bank account this morning with a note."

"$35 million, right? Yeah, it's my inheritance from my grandfather. All is okay. Can you put that into a protective account until I can come down and discuss how I would like to manage that? Thank you, Ben. We will be in touch."

I hang up and sigh. "My father was trying to kill me for that inheritance my supposed grandfather left for me and not him...it's a very long and complicated story." He gets off my bed. "Another day for that, you eat and gather up your strength. Lyric would kill us if she saw you looking ragged and unkempt and I know to never piss off a pregnant lady. I'll be back in a few hours and we can go back before dinner."

I shake my head to clear it from all the past craziness and dig into my food. Afterward, I lie down and say a little prayer of protection for my girl and my child. I didn't realize how fast I fell asleep until I woke up five hours later. I go to brush my teeth and Cheetah knocks before coming in and I peek out.

"We checked on you after three hours, but you were so tired, we needed you to get as much as possible. Hope you're not too upset at us; we've been keeping tabs on her and Digi and not much has changed. If it had, we would have woken you up.

"It's fine, I know you would have, and you were right I needed to rest. I'll be ready to head out soon."

"Okay."

We made it back by 6 pm and the others left to get dinner and rest up. They'd be back in the morning. I went to the gift shop and bought her a dozen long-stemmed red roses and a teddy bear that read "Congratulations". I brought a small overnight bag and sprayed the bear with my favorite cologne I only wore when she was around. I thought the familiar aroma may wake her up sooner. I brought my blanket I kept on my recliner and laid it over her. I wanted familiarity around her when she woke up.

I turn on the tv for background noise as I pull a chair up next to her sweet face. I kissed her temple, "I'm back baby, they made me go home, shower, eat, and rest but I was so eager to get back to you..." I rest my hand on her stomach and the fetal monitoring band, "and our bundle of joy. I still can't believe it. You've made me the happiest man ever. Who knew a little firecracker like you would change my life forever? I know this is my mom's doing because she always wanted me to not dwell on her death, so she sent me an angel. Thanks, mom."

A small knock and the doctor comes in. "Hello, Mr. McElroy, you look well-rested. I'm glad to see."

"Yeah, forced rest. How is she, doc?"

"Well, the most powerful medications should have exited her system. She should be awake some time soon. I am going to have Dr. Hall, who is the OB/GYN, come in and do an ultrasound once she is awake. I'll have the nurse bring in a pillow and blanket for you. The cafeteria is open 24 hours, Mr. McElroy. Take care of yourself."

Lyric

Soooo bored! All I'm doing is floating and thinking, living in the past when I am ready for my future. This is torture! I just want to go...

Something within the darkness pulled me; however, the darkness lessened, transitioning from pitch black to dark gray. A faint light emerged.

Oh, please let this be my life and not heaven.

Then, in a flash, my eyes slowly open and my surroundings are dark except for the neon glow of the television. My head is all fuzzy as my eyes adjust. Definitely a hospital room, but I recognized a familiar scent. It was a manly scent, and I knew it anywhere. It was his scent, but he wasn't near. Sitting up on my elbows, I see my love asleep in a small recliner, his giant frame barely covered by a thin blanket, his head resting on a pillow that looked far too small and uncomfortable.

I slid back to lying down, that little movement drained all my energy, and I huffed loudly.

"Aleister." It came out as a straggled whisper. My throat was sore, but I really wanted to see my love. I cleared my throat and tried it again.

"Aleister!" This time it came out with my voice and he

stirred a bit. He must be exhausted. I gather my strength to sit up and this time I grab a plastic cup from my food tray and throw it in his direction. The oddly loud noise it makes wakes him and he sits up. A confused "Huh? What...?" escaped his lips as he tried to comprehend what was happening. Then, faster than I could react, he appeared beside me; tears still blurring my vision.

"Oh God, I missed you so much." He kissed me from my forehead to my lips and I couldn't help but laugh until I started coughing. He pours some water and uses the remote to angle me upward.

The water felt so refreshing. "What day is it? What time is it?"

He checks his watch. "It's 10 pm and you've been here five almost six days."

"What! I've been here almost a week? Oh my gosh, I missed your birthday!" I pout, and he chuckles.

"I have no desire to celebrate my birthday anymore, especially after this one." He smiles and points to the roses, which were absolutely beautiful, and then he hands me a teddy bear. 'Congratulations,' it read, but I was confused. Maybe that's all he could find.

"Thank you, they're beautiful." I whispered, because he was so close. The scent of his beard, a musky blend of sandalwood and something else indefinably masculine, filled my senses as I pulled him close for a sweet kiss.

"Where is everyone?"

"Well, Knox and Cheetah are in Digi's room and the rest went home for the night. They'll be back in the morning. I can tell them you're awake and I'm sure they'll come right back."

"No, no, no, I'll see them soon."

A cheery nurse comes in and walks over to me with a bright smile. "Oh, hello! I'm Nurse Eve. I'll be taking care of you, Miss Pullman. I'm glad to see you're awake. Typically, when a loved one is close by, it encourages them to come around. Let's get your vitals, okay?"

I give her a small smile as she checks my IV bag, my blood pressure, respiration, temperature, and heart rate. She flashes my eyes with a mini flashlight, and I blink rapidly.

"Good. All your vitals seem to be normal. Are you in any physical pain?"

"Nothing I can't handle. Oh, except for this tight band around my stomach. What's that for?" I tap the plastic circle disk at the top and I notice the numbers on the monitor fluc- tuate before returning to normal.

"Oh, it's to monitor the baby's vitals, sweetie!"

She smiled, continuing to write on the clipboard, as I stared, speechless, at Aleister.

"W-wha-what did she just say?" I felt the tears collect as he took my hand and a growing smile forms across his face.

"Aleister...am I?"

He nods his head. "Yes, my sweet Lyric, you're pregnant with our baby. I am so excited and so are the guys. That's why I gave you that." He points to the teddy bear in my hand. Now it makes sense.

Cupid

My beautiful girl was shocked speechless at the confir- mation of her pregnancy. I took my hand and pushed her jaw up so she would close her mouth. As soon as it does, the tears fall and she hugs the teddy bear tightly. "Oh, my gosh! I'm pregnant."

Eve hugs her and smiles. "You sound like me when I found out about my first child. Congrats to you both. Listen, if you need anything, push the call button. I'm here until 9 am. Get some rest and breakfast will come around 8 am. You take good care of her, dad."

"Absolutely." The nurse leaves, and she openly starts bawling. "I'm pregnant!"

"Are you happy or sad? I can't really tell."

She laughs and wipes her tears. "I'm so unbelievably happy! I'm glad that he or she didn't get hurt after... after..." I place my hand on her stomach.

"Shhh, no talk about that. I need mommy and baby to rest and we'll talk more in the morning. I brought you my blanket so you can sleep better, and the teddy bear has my scent."

"I know. I recognized it instantly. Sleep in bed with me?" She slides over, leaving barely enough for me to fit a leg in. "Kitten, I don't think I fit."

"You will, I promise. I need your touch to comfort me, please?"

Those beautiful, bright blue eyes looked at me with hopeful expectation. I sigh and resign to the fact that this may be an uncomfortable night of rest for me, but anything for her. I take off my shoes and t-shirt, leaving my sweatpants on and climbing in.

I was about to get in when she shifted, half her body covering me, so I slid the rest of the way and became her extra pillow. She adjusted, so the band was resting comfortably on her stomach but not jabbing into me. I focused on the sound of the sonar that was the baby's heartbeat. I could sleep listening to that alone. Knowing there is a little being that we created between us is still a shock.

I kiss her forehead as I rub her back, and she is asleep in no time. Her snores are soothing and eventually, I sleep the best I have in weeks.

Lyric

I'm pregnant! The sheer joy is unbelievable; I feel like I'm floating on air. I stare up at the sleeping giant and smile. I sketched circles on his chest, then gently touched his lips, wanting to feel them once more. I'm surprised when I feel his lips pucker to kiss my fingertips. It sends tingles down my spine and I know I'm blushing so badly, but it doesn't matter.

"Morning, kitten." He leans down and his lips, feather-light, brush against mine in a soft kiss. I really missed everything about him.

"Morning. I hope you weren't too uncomfortable, but I slept so much better with you here. Thank you."

Before he could kiss me again, the door opened to the entire club, and they were now standing in the room.

"Oh jeez, do you guys ever stop?! We already got our first biker baby." Blondie laughs as he presents a dozen sunflowers in a matching yellow vase placing them next to my love's roses.

"Aww, you didn't have to bring me flowers!"

Next thing I know, they all present fresh flowers, from peonies to gardenias to tulips!

"Well, we can't take them back now. We are so glad you are awake and healing. We missed you, but that guy there definitely missed you the most."

Aleister squeezes my side, confirming what I already knew. I sat up a bit more while I watched my food tray and dresser fill with flowers and the aroma was the perfect mix. Everyone sits down, but I notice Knox step outside.

Jackal is at the end of my bed and smiling wildly. I don't think I've ever seen this group so damn happy. He squeezes my feet and I raise my brow.

"What has gotten into you guys?"

Laughter erupted as they exchanged glances, then Jackal exclaimed, "Are you kidding me?" That little miracle in there survived being shot and its mama survived to make sure the baby had a home to grow in. That is a strength I've never seen before; the miracle of pregnancy and impending birth is fascinating to this group of old rough and tumble guys. It's our first biker baby. Can't wait to present the baby's first cut."

They all laugh. "But what if it's a girl?" I raise my brow.

"Then she'll be our first biker babe." The words hung in the air, a mixture of excitement and a hint of mischief. I punch Aleister in the arm. "Hey, I thought that was my position?" He kisses my forehead. "You're so much more than that."

Knox comes back into the room with his back facing me as he pulls something in. He turns around and I see Digi smiling so hard.

"Lyric!"

"Digi!"

He maneuvers the wheelchair as close as he can, then

slowly rises so he can lean over and give me a really tight hug. I readjust the band before I lay down again.

"I missed you, too munchkin, but don't squeeze too hard." I say as I inhale deeper than usual.

He jumps back a bit. "I'm sorry did I hurt you?" He watches as I shift and lean up against Aleister.

I take his hand and squeeze. "No, but do you hear that sound, sounds like a radar or sonar? Do you know what it is?" He shakes his head; I can see his wheels turning, trying to figure it out.

"Well, it monitors the baby's heartbeat...you're going to be a big brother." His eyes widen and he gasps. "Oh, you're pregnant?! Big brother? Me?"

I tell him to sit. "Of course, you've been the closest to a little brother I've had since my own brothers grew up and moved away. I remember our conversation about you wanting a genuine family. Digi, you are my family and no matter what happens, I want you with me, with us. What do you say?"

A grin stretched across his face as he struggled to hold back his excitement. Aleister smiles. "I agree. I want you to follow us wherever we may go."

Digi hugs me and then walks around slowly and hugs Aleister. "I want nothing more than to have a family. I mean I have you all as my family, but I also wanted a real mom and dad type family. I never had that."

He looks back and blushes, hoping not to hurt anyone's feelings. Jackal squeezes his hand, reassuring him. "We know what you meant, son. Now you have two families who love and adore you. Speaking of plans, have you two discussed that? What's next?"

I shrug my shoulders, realizing I've only been conscious

for a day. I haven't sorted out my life in that time. "Not really. I mean I have a substantial amount of money left from Dave and we could live comfortably for a while..."

Suddenly, they all start laughing. It's so loud, but I'm left in the dark.

"What's so funny?"

Aleister squeezes me to grab my attention. "Don't you remember my dad tried to kill me for my inheritance on my 30th? Well, I got it... all $35 million."

My jaw dropped.

Cupid

Her mouth fell open and I think she squeaked. "Kitten? Are you okay?"

"M-millions?! You're telling me you are now a multi-millionaire?"

"More like *we* all are. I plan to keep $15 million and split the rest equally among the group, if that's okay with you?"

"Why wouldn't it be? It's your money."

I turned her face towards me. "It's *our* money, but honestly, what was I going to do with the entire amount? People change or become greedy. I don't want it to change me. I would rather share it with my family, who was always there for me." She smiles and wraps her arms around me. "Okay."

With that settled, another knock came. I thought it was the nurse, but I was wrong. It was the sheriff's department.

"Miss Pullman, can we have a moment of your time to get your witness statement?"

The guys file out, heading to Digi's room to wait.

"Can he stay?" She asks while pointing to me and they agree, so I put on my t-shirt for decency.

She clearly recalled everything from her arrival at her hotel room to the moment of the shooting.

She even recounted Trix's confrontation, Johnny's vicious attack and his threats to rape her and even my father, visiting her in the bar. Her memory is impressive; she recalled details I'd forgotten, likely because my anger clouded my mind.

Her calmness made for a strong testimony against all of them. She even gave them the combination to the bank safe where she stashed the video surveillance against Johnny. He was going to rot in that jail for the drug charges alone, but now for Dave's murder. Hopefully, he would die there.

At the conclusion, the police officers relayed the latest information. Trix pleaded no contest and in return for testifying against Johnny and my dad, they gave her a deal. Ten years for arson and aggravated assault. I knew that slimy bitch was responsible.

The officers delivered some interesting news: my father had been castrated. Cheetah's bullet had lodged in his spine, paralyzing him from the waist down.

Prosecutors will charge him with over 45 counts related to drug trafficking, distribution, possession of gun caches, assault, felony assault, and more. They also revealed he may be charged with 12 murders of cartel members and drug mules who died during transactions or smuggling drugs in and out of the country.

That was a lot to take in, but she did so in stride. Afterwards, they tell us they will keep in touch. She sighs heavily once they leave, and that's when the nurse comes in. "Just checking up on mama and baby. Hmmm... your numbers are a little high. I want you to listen to some music and take 30 minutes concentrating on your breathing to relax. Can you do that?"

She snuggled close, her soft hair brushing my arm, and I pulled out my phone to play some calming music. A torrential downpour, punctuated by the deep rumble of thunder, blended with the melodic notes of an Indian flute, forming a soothing environment. The nurse nods and mouths a thank you as she dims the lights and I rub her back, listening to her breathing.

I used my free hand to text the guys to give us half an hour before they return. She moans and then sighs; I felt a stir within me thinking about how warm she feels. About how much I want to feel her other warmth wrapped around me. Squeezing me so deliciously until I...

"Baby?" She says but is still resting with her eyes closed.

I try to calm my thoughts and breathing. "Yes?"

"What are we going to do after I get released?"

"We can do whatever we want, anywhere you want, whenever you want. Don't worry about that right now. I need you to rest so the baby can relax."

She rubs her non-existent stomach. "What do you wish for?"

"Doesn't matter. He or she won't be the only one."

She gasps as I press my lips to her temple. "Says you...you don't have to pop them out of your vagina." She giggles, warranting another tender kiss.

"You're right, but I'll be with you every step of the way."

"Uh-huh," she replied, unconvinced.

The next half hour went by in comfortable silence.

Lyric

I spent another four days in the hospital as they tended to my surgical incisions and kept watch of my little nugget.

I got an ultrasound yesterday and watched Aleister weep when she handed him a copy of the sonogram. It was so touching, he promptly placed it in his wallet like a proud dad. He'd plaster copies of it all over his room, probably the house, if he could. He was over the moon.

Later that day, I finally got my walking papers, along with after care instructions and medications. Aleister packs all the items he brought and my things and I see a car outside. He rented it to pick me up so I can rest comfortably.

We slowed down as we neared the hotel. I watched the rest of the family head back to the house. "Hey, what are we doing? Are we not going back to the clubhouse?" He parks the car and grabs the bag, helping me out of the car slowly. We walk into the hotel and up to the front desk. A tall blonde looks up and greets us with a beautiful smile. "Oh. Mr. McElroy, we have your suite all set up, following your instructions to the letter. Hello, is this your wife?" He nods, and she smiles, "Congratulations on the bundle of joy! You look beautiful."

Oh gosh, I'm blushing. I feel it radiating off my skin. "Thank you."

She hands him the keys. They are sleek black with gold chips in them. "So, as discussed, you are the only person on that floor, and you have private access to the elevator over here just tap your card to access it. Only your cards and the backup here work. If you call and give us a name, we will give them a temporary card they must check in and check out. The security cameras are 24/7 and we are available at any time. Is there anything else that I can do for you?"

"No, Katherine. That's all, thank you. The little lady and baby need some rest."

The main elevators hummed with activity, but we walked to a single, quieter elevator, its faint mechanical whir the only sound. I was curious at what he had put together. We step in and he hits the PH button. "Penthouse?" He just smiles as the elevator goes until the floor indicator light goes out and the door opens. The door is directly in front and he taps the card and holds the door open as I duck under to enter the room.

I step in and stop. "Oh...Aleister...it's..."

Wow, these hormones are crazy! I'm crying like a baby at all the roses; white, pink, and red everywhere! Vases and vases and vases! I'm wandering around, just breathing in the incredible scent. It's so beautiful and romantic, completely unexpected from someone who couldn't even say he liked me a week ago. I turn to thank him, and then I'm completely surprised when his front caresses my back ever so gently. I can feel his body heat, among other things.

He spins me around. With a serious face, he took my hand and stroked my cheek. "I'm sorry Lyric, it shouldn't have taken almost losing you for me to tell you how I felt. I was stubborn and stupid and all I want to do is make it up to you and prove that yes... I love you. You have my heart, soul and you're carrying our future. I never want you to doubt how much you mean to me." He drops to his knees and nuzzles my stomach and kisses it gently.

I couldn't help but giggle when his lips tickled me, a featherlight touch. Then there was a silence, not uncomfortable but charged with a vibrant energy that hummed in the air. I know what he's thinking, to be gentle, to be mindful of my wound, and not be as aggressive. But I know what I wanted and how I wanted it.

He looks up at me, and I bite my lip. A searing heat blossoms in my core, making me feel flushed and breathless.. Nothing like the combination of wanton lust, raging hormones, and a very sexy pierced and tattooed bad boy biker at your feet begging for forgiveness.

It just does things to you.

And I want those things done to me now.

He stands up and now towers over me once again. His fingers, warm and gentle, brush my cheek, drawing a soft sigh as I lean into his touch. He bends, the scent of his cologne, a musky, familiar comfort filling my senses, before his lips claim mine in a hungry kiss, a carnal need fulfilled. I desperately needed his touch in any and every way.

"Jump."

I eagerly hop up, and his powerful arms hold me against his core. I was wearing black leggings, no underwear, and one of his shirts. The sensation of his hardness against my hot and wet core elicited a moan that I couldn't stifle, our eyes meeting in a charged exchange.

"Is my kitten needy?"

"So much...please."

He guides us back to the bedroom, the plush carpet soft beneath his feet. I stand on the velvet ottoman, the cool fabric against my feet. Leaning down, the scent of his skin fills my senses as he unbuckles his belt, the metallic click echoing softly. His jeans and boxers fall to the floor with a muffled thud, followed by his tank top.

He playfully kisses below my navel as I shed my shirt,

because that's what's accessible to him with me standing on this pedestal.

I see a flash of concern as he eyes the small bandage covering my surgical wound. He didn't want to hurt me. I was fortunate to get top care and medications, so I was healing fast. I tried to distract him upward as I reached around and unhooked my bra. He slid his hands upward and covered my breasts where my bra once was. His warm, rough hands and thick fingers feel magical against them. He gets carried away and squeezes harder than usual, and I yelp.

"Oh, sorry. You're going to be sensitive because they're growing to make room for the milk production."

I raise my brow and stare at him.

"I bought an expectant mother's book and read a few chapters about the early months of pregnancy while you were still unconscious. It's pretty interesting. I have it in my bag if you want to read it?"

I smirk at him, "Not at this very moment, no. I need you to take care of more pressing matters, like I haven't had a good orgasm in weeks."

He growls as he pushes me, and I fall to the bed.

Cupid

My little kitten is blunt. She needs relief; she needs to cum, and I'm about to make it my mission to make up for lost time. I know she can see my concern involving her wound, but she assures me she is not in any pain and will tell me if she is.

I tower over her and grip her leggings with my teeth and pull down while growling. She laughs at the absurdity. I missed her laughs.

I get them off and toss them somewhere as I kiss her feet, ankles, working my way north. As soon as she can reach, her fingers are in my hair, pulling lightly. I know the intensity will change once I'm feasting on what's mine.

I tease, slowing down when I get to her upper thighs, kissing across instead of upward.

"Cupid, stop teasing me..." I looked up, but her eyes were closed. She's lucky. I'll let her slide this time. She calls me by name, not my club name. Although that sounds magical too. I'll come back to that. Right now, I want her writhing underneath me.

Every inch of her was flawless, and she was even sweeter

on my tongue. A tantalizing scent filled the air, and the taste of her lingered on my lips. I read that the chemistry could change the scent and taste. I could eat her for dessert.

I'm thrown back into reality when her hand tightens deep in my hair. "Oh, baby." She purred as she arched her back, pushing me in further.

Whatever you want, sunshine.

Lost in the moment, I delve in deeper and before I know it, she's convulsing, and her sweet scent enveloping me. I lick it up and look up to see her trying to catch her breath.

We're not even close to being done.

Lyric

I couldn't stop that orgasm if I wanted to, but I didn't. The release was earth-shattering, and I felt like I was float-ing. It was like ten orgasms in one. I turn to my side as he spoons me, running his fingers along my arm.

It's hard to keep my eyes open, and then I yawn.

I think...

Yup, it's happening...

I'm... falling asleep...zzz.

Cupid

What... the hell?! Her snoring was almost instant. I read that fatigue can happen, but come on!

Now I have a hard-on and a sleeping beauty. I pull the covers over us and I spoon her, kissing her shoulder. I slide my arrow between her cheeks and nod off.

Hopefully, it'll go down. Still, I'd rather be nowhere else.

Lyric

I fell asleep... before sex. Who does that?!

I suppose I was more tired than I thought. Then that orgasm took me out. I needed relief, and it felt magical! I go to stretch, but careful because he's nuzzled behind me. Is that? I reach around and feel... Yup, his dick is resting between me. I check the clock. It's been almost two hours. How is he not soft yet? He must be fantasizing, that's kind of hot.

Knowing how close it is made me so wet, I rock back and forth, trying not to wake him. The friction feels so good... I look back and he's still asleep. I palm my breast with one hand while trying to hold myself up with the other.

"Mmm... fuck..." I saw no movement from him, so I adjusted him and moved back, feeling filled as my walls throbbed with him inside me. I rock back and forth slowly; with every stroke, I get wetter and wetter.

I've never felt so sensitive, must be the hormones. I purr, reacting to the motion, and I continue to palm my breasts, tweaking them alternately.

His hands, suddenly clamping around my waist, pull me hard against him. The rough impact of his chest against my back is jarring. He sits up, his breath warm on my skin as he nibbles at my shoulder. A light, insistent pressure.

"What a delicious way to wake up. I swore I was having an intense wet dream until I peek to see me sliding in and out of you so teasingly. You're in so much trouble, your kitten must be punished."

Uh oh.

He's not talking about me and it's confirmed when he pulls my leg up and back towards my chest. His other hand teases my clit, my entire body flushes, and I gasp loudly.

Oh god, he feels so damn good.

"Faster, baby, please." The words were a breathless whisper as he aggressively showed me how much he missed me. He bites my shoulder, then whispers in my ear. "I'm running this show, got it?"

A shiver of excitement courses through my body as his movements become faster and more intense. All I could do was moan his name; the sound was raw, desperate, and the only thing that felt real in that moment.

He lets go of my leg but quickly flips us and now I'm straddling his lap. He feels even bigger and deeper.

His hand comes down perfectly, swatting my ass in succession as he eyes me, licking his lips. "Mmm, oh fuck..."

"Ride me. Now." His expression is dead serious.

Why does that turn me on more?!

The rhythm of my swaying body intensifies as his hands tighten around my hips.

"Oh baby, I missed feeling you. You're so tight. Shit, I won't last long if you keep doing that, kitten." I switched the direction to up and down and that may have cut the time in half now he was thrusting against me. The counter motion had him hitting my G spot perfectly. I may not make it another minute.

Our moans, pants, and gasps filled the air, a symphony of passion sealing our bond. The knot in my abdomen unraveled, and it was explosive as I screamed out my orgasm.

"Oh... I'm... ahhh!" I dug my nails in his chest and clenched my wall muscles tight as I came.

"Fuck kitten! Shit... oh shit, I'm..." He grunted as he pulled me down and thrust upward as he came. For good measure, I twisted his nipple piercings.

"Fuck, baby, yes!" I swear he came twice once I did that, or maybe it was just a lot from lack of sex? It *had* been awhile. Who knows? Hell, who cares. I was already knocked up.

I collapsed onto his chest, the steady beat of his heart a soothing rhythm against my ear as his arms held me tightly and his kiss landed softly on my forehead.

"I'm hungry."

He laughs. "And I love you, too. Let's get mommy and baby fed." He orders room service while I hop in the shower. He avoids joining this time because we would never get the food. I come out and he's checking his piercings in the mirror.

"Are you okay? Did I take it too far?" He looked down to see me in just a short black robe that was on the hook.

He pulls me in. "No, they were loosening anyway, so I tightened them as much as I could. I'll have my piercer tighten them just to be sure."

"Can I come? I always wanted to get a piercing. Maybe I'll do it then."

"Pierce what, like your tongue or nipples?"

I smirk as I walk to the door that leads to the living room.

I gesture my eyes downward, "Lower..." And I left him shocked.

Cupid

Holy shit! We just finished, but she wants another performance. I groan as I follow her out and she's searching through movie selections.

I had to be sure, "How much lower? Like your belly button?"

She giggles with hooded eyes. "You know that's not what I meant. I had my nipples pierced, but I didn't like it. I liked the sensation, so I wanted to see what it would be like to pierce my clit. I think it'll make my pussy super sensitive."

I feel the jealousy beginning to form. "So, you want me to be okay with some guy looking, touching, piercing what's mine? And won't it hurt during childbirth?"

"Sweetheart, it'll make it more sensitive to your touch, and if properly done, I won't have to remove it. Pretty please, Cupid?" She gave me the doe eyes; I felt my resolve melt.

"Fine, but I'm there at all times."

"Thank you! Thank goodness I kept up with my Brazilian wax appointments." She trails off as she cuddles up to me. I'm a throbbing mess.

"Hey, you never told me why you brought us here instead of to the clubhouse?" She presses enter on the remote and a movie starts.

"I moved out and made a temporary home here while we figure out what the next steps are. I had the hotel salvage most of the stuff from your old room. We needed a quiet place to focus on finding a dream location, a house, and all that stuff."

"What about the club? I don't want to leave them. My little nugget has a family, and I don't want them to miss out." She rubs her stomach.

"I don't think that will be a problem, since everyone has a substantial amount of money. We've discussed moving the entire club for a while now. All the pieces seem to be falling together. All we have to do is pick a location."

"Oh, San Diego! Please, baby? It's my dream location and there's so much to do and the club will fit in. There are so many clubs already. We can stroll the pier with both the kids and watch Digi play big brother and get a puppy! Please, please, please?!"

If she only knew how much I wanted to give her everything she desired, she wouldn't have had to ask. She's bouncing up and down on the couch. Her breasts look amazing. It's really hard to focus.

"Aleister!"

Oops, caught.

I snap out of it. "Then I guess we're going to California. We can talk about details later. Let's head to the clubhouse to discuss. It's almost time for church, anyway."

"I thought there were no women allowed?"

"No, no club bunnies around. You're my ol' lady, full access. Come on, let's get ready to go."

Lyric

We change and get dressed to go to the clubhouse for church.

I follow him in and find myself bombarded by overbearing bikers. "Lyric, sit down. We'll bring you something to drink and eat. Here's a pillow..."

Oh my gosh, they're so adorable and annoying at the same time.

"Guys! I'm not about to give birth, relax. Hold your meeting, as usual. If I need something, I promise I'll ask."

Jackal bangs the gavel, "Alright, this is the first church we've had since the whole fiasco. We are still awaiting any additional information from the police department, but I found out that all parties at the compound will face four additional attempted murder charges for holding everyone hostage."

I was a bit confused. "Four? It was us and Digi. Who's the fourth?"

Cupid rubs my stomach and smiles. "Four, baby."

"I told the cops when they called me in for additional

information that you were pregnant and the horrible conditions you were in, along with the extreme stress they put you through. I tried to get them to add child neglect, but he said it was a stretch. But the additional charges add time on all their sentences, even Trixie with her plea deal."

Good. Worthless bitch.

She burned down my place because he wanted me and not her. As if that would have made him come running back. I guess good dick will cloud your judgment.

"Anyway, let's discuss the big news. Our brother Cupid has offered to split his inheritance with his brothers, and now I open up the floor for a discussion of improvements."

Cheetah stands. "Well, I know we all thank our brother for being so generous. I propose we vote where to move. Something we've discussed for years. It's time to change the scenery for this club! I assume no one wants to separate, right?"

I look and they all nod. Cupid stands. "I would never leave the family behind, besides this little lady has a dream location. I want to put it up for a vote. San Diego, California, now to make a point..."

"No need, all in favor?"

AYE!

It was unanimous, and I found my eyes wet with tears.

Damn these hormones!

Hey! I can blame my pregnancy for anything!

"Well, that was easy enough. We will work out details of the move date, travel route, housing search for the new clubhouse. Of course, no one has to stay in the new clubhouse, but we have to agree on a centralized location. Cupid and Lyric, I expect you to have a separate home to raise your family. Digi, I need you to look up what it takes to transfer the club's charter from state to state. Well, men, we got a lot of work to do as a club and individually. Church dismissed."

He bangs his gavel, and I exhale in relief.

"Digi, sweetheart, come here."

He sits beside me, and I take his warm hand in mine. "I know you're an adult and of age with a fortune, but if you want, I'd still like you to live with us." He looked even more surprised than the last time.

"Really? I thought that maybe with the new baby you'd be too busy for me and I am an adult."

I shake my head and smile. "Never. You'll always be as important as the baby. We want to be the family you always wanted." I look behind me and Aleister nods in agreement.

He nudges Digi's shoulder, "You know how I feel about ya kiddo, no matter the relation, brother or son, we're family."

Next thing I know, Digi hops over me to pummel Cupid in a hug. I slide over to avoid getting kicked.

It was a sweet sight, my son and my... hey...

"Uh, excuse me, not to break up the tender moment, but you and I have something to discuss, sir. Follow me."

Cupid

She waves her fingers for me to follow her out to the backyard.

Escaping the noisy house, she turned, her expression and crossed arms making me uneasy.

Shit.

I quickly try to recall if I said anything to upset her.

"Aleister... What are we? What is this?" She motions with her fingers between us.

UGH, why do women need to ask this question? Considering everything, I understand why she asked the question. I barely told her I liked her but could sleep with her. She's carrying my son or daughter; she holds my heart. I was a mess; she deserves the world.

"What are we? We are a family. You are my girl, my feisty kitten, and my future wife. I want to show you every day just how much you mean to me. I'll never hold back from you again. And when I find the perfect ring, I'll drop to my knee and profess my undying love for you. Does that answer your question?"

She sits on my bended knee and wraps her arms around me and quietly sobs. She draws back and smiles. "It was perfect."

Lyric

Several days later, the club celebrated with a lively BBQ; the air filled with the smell of grilling meat and laughter. On this beautiful day, they set out picnic tables in the backyard. Although it was windy, the men continued to play football. It's amazing they will keep their cuts on for everything, even though they were sweating up a storm. It's dedication to their brotherhood.

I sit at the table because the wind will surely blow my robin egg blue sundress up. Besides, I love watching them. Jackal's at the grill with Club, bringing him the meats and whipping up all the side dishes. I offered to help, but they banished me from the kitchen. I swear they think I'm about to go into labor and I'm barely two months along. No matter, I love my family, even their over protectiveness.

I feel a rush of air, then a kiss on my shoulder. I look up to see my boyfriend smiling. I told him happiness looks good on him; he says he has me to thank.

Who knew that being abandoned in this forgotten corner of the world would place me right where I needed to be?

He sits sideways so he can slide me close to him, wrapping his arms around me.

OH GOD! I didn't think to check the window, he usually never opens it, why is it open now?! And then I found out they were airing out the house.

Shoot me. Shoot me now... my cheeks must be glowing red.

"Oh, my god..." I bury my face in my hands.

First a chuckle, then another, and soon they were all in stitches.

"Now we know HOW it happened." Cheetah says as they all fall out around the room. I turn and look. Even Aleister's laughing.

I cross my arms. He pulled me close, a smile playing on his lips as he kissed my forehead. I pout, "That's not funny!"

"They're teasing. We've all heard each other have sex."

"Correction, we've heard casual sex before. That was... intense!"

I bury myself into his side. Can the earth just swallow me whole, please?!

He kisses my forehead and squeezes my side. "Alright guys, enough. We're heading home. I'm sure you can continue to have fun without us."

I sigh in relief. "Hey Digi, you want to come with us? There's a second bedroom. We can have a movie night together?"

I wanted to get him comfortable being around us in a family environment. I couldn't help but laugh at how fast he ran upstairs.

I've seen that kid's room. It may be awhile. He's a total mess, a typical teenager who never cleans. No doubt he is currently throwing things in his bag. Hope that includes enough underwear. He was excited, and seeing joy on his face was most important.

A few minutes later, he came down with his duffle bag, and, of course, his trusty laptop.

"I'm ready!" Digi ties his bag on his bike, and we head to the hotel.

After entering the suite, I showered and changed while Cupid ordered room service. Digi was constantly eating, while I had eaten nothing since I got sick. I made sure he knew to avoid my current triggers, pickles, olives, mayo, and red onion.

Cupid

Digi went to put his things in his room; if all went as planned, he would stay with us until our big move. It's not as shocking for me to play the dad role since I've had him under my wing. The only change is he went from club brother to my son.

He comes out at the same time she does. She's wearing her royal blue pajama bottoms and a white crop top. She barely had a bump, but I noticed the minute change and I smiled.

She sits on one side of me and him on the other. He's fidgeting and rubbing his hands. I've known him long enough to know something important is on his mind.

Lyric speaks first. "Hey, whatever you want to say, you can. You're safe with us, okay?"

He smiles, "I-I wanted to know if I could call you mom and dad? I was always in foster care and they didn't deserve to be called that. They treated me so terribly. I feel comfortable calling you that, but only if you're okay with that."

He trailed off, a nervous energy radiating from him as he

waited to see if we'd say yes. I look over because I hear sniffling and she's in tears before she climbs over me to hug him.

"Of course, sweetheart, being your mother would be such
an honor. This means the world to me, and I love you,
kiddo!"

Now he's sniffling. His eyes brightened as he looked at
her. "Okay...mom." Lyric bursts out crying while hugging our
son, who was way taller than her but still on the scrawny
side. Guess I'll have to bulk him up. I mean I am his dad.

Then it hit me, a powerful wave of emotion, a deep sense
of connection, more than just our brotherhood. I am this kid's
dad. In just a few months, I transitioned from bachelorhood
to family life. If you would have said that this was my future,
I'd probably laugh in your face, but here we are.

A knock came at the door, so I answered it. The bellhop
brings our meal, and I give him a generous tip. I place the
plates on the table in front of us as they calm down from
their crying fest. It was sweet, to be honest.

I sat down; two pairs of eyes fixed on me. Oh, I realize
now that I was supposed to answer. I pat her leg and she
moves to the other side, so it's me sitting next to Digi. He's
biting his lip, eager for my response. I see him start to fidget
and fiddle with his fingers.

"Come here, son." I pull him close, his lanky body
melting against mine in a sigh of relief. A soft, broken sob
reaches my ear. Eventually, he sits back and smiles.
"Thanks...dad."

"No problem, kiddo. Now pick a movie so we can watch
together as a family. He scans the movie titles. I'm pleasantly
surprised when she tugs my beard to get me to face her and
gives me the sweetest kiss.

"Thank you, baby. You're going to be an amazing father."

"Anything for you, kitten." I pepper her face with kisses.

"Mom! Dad! Please."

The sound of our laughter fills the room, a warm wave washing over us. I sink into the soft cushions of the couch, my love's warm body pressed against my side, my son nestled close on the other, munching on nacho chips, a comforting rhythm.

A perfect way to end the night.

Lyric

Surprise, surprise. I fell asleep. I barely remember the first 20 minutes of the first movie. My nugget is wearing me out. I wake up in bed with a hefty arm around me. I glance over to see the time: 7:00 am. I felt so refreshed. I try to maneuver my way from under this tree trunk of an arm, especially because he's laying right on my little nugget and I really don't need a bout of morning sickness. I shift his arm over and the movement causes him to roll over and sigh.

Thank goodness.

I stretch and go into the bathroom to do my routine. I come out and he's still snoring.

I open the door to the living space and Digi's on his computer playing some first-person shooter game I don't recognize.

"Morning, mom."

Good grief, don't cry every time he calls you that, Lyric, get it together.

I bent down, kissed his forehead gently, then sat next to him. "Morning, sweetheart."

His smile is infectious. "Last night, I dreamt we were all together on the beach, taking family photos. It felt so real!

I mussed his hair. "And it will be. Once we're settled, we'll take those photos, well, once he or she is born, and we find our cute little dog. I'm glad you had such a wonderful dream. Sorry I fell asleep last night, pregnancy is draining and a learning experience, I tell you. Are you hungry?"

"I could eat." Typical response. I grabbed the menu to browse the breakfast options, and I heard rumbling from my room.

"Hmm, your father must be up." As soon as I spoke those words, a wave of emotion washed over me, and I couldn't stop crying.

I am a mess.

"Are you okay? Is this a pregnancy thing or did I say something wrong?" He looked genuinely concerned, but I smiled through the tears. "No, it just touched me to hear me call him your father. It's silly, I know."

I rubbed my tiny bump while still ruffling his hair. He shrugs his shoulders. "To be honest, I cried last night before bed, the happiest I've ever been. I love my brothers, of course, but this is a dream come true."

I wrap my arms around him, and I hear a sigh. "Must you guys be so adorably sweet this early in the morning? Morning son, morning kitten."

I almost burst out in tears again. He said it so naturally that my heart melted. He sat next to me and perused the menu until there was a knock on the door.

He looked at me. "Did you order already?"

"No, we were looking at the menu."

He gets up and opens the door. "Oh, hey, come in."

I look to see his grandfather with a medium-sized gift box.

"Good morning, I apologize for coming early but I came bearing gifts!"

Cupid

I opened the door to see grandpa and promptly let him in. I forgot he texted he was stopping by in the morning, so I gave the concierge his name to let him up. I let him know Digi was here as well, and he said that it was perfect and didn't need to make an extra trip. I have no idea what he meant.

In chinos and a blue checked shirt, he was as casually dressed as much as a wealthy man could be. Seeing him, I realized I might age well. He was remarkably spry for his age.

He notices my family. "Good morning, I apologize for coming early but I came bearing gifts." He says as he holds the medium size box.

"It's okay, we were all up. You didn't have to bring us anything."

He tsks as he sits in the chair by the couch, handing the box to Lyric. "I wanted to. I'm not trying to buy affection. I want to celebrate welcoming you to my family while celebrating your newly formed one. So, open the box." He smiled eagerly as Lyric removed the top. I sat down as she pulled out a small box with my name, one with hers, one for Digi, and one labeled for the baby.

Lyric's fingers, trembling with anticipation, fumbled with the ribbon. The box sprang open with a delicate click, releasing the scent of aged velvet. A gasp escaped her lips as she saw the gleaming silver bracelet, its charms tinkling softly. A heart-shaped charm, biggest of all, dominated the others; engraved upon it, the word 'Mom' shone, catching the light. There was also a motorcycle charm, a musical note for her name, and a little home charm.

"It's beautiful, thank you." I clasp it to her wrist; she shakes it and smiles. He nods, pleased at her approval.

Digi lifts the lid of his box, revealing a gleaming silver watch, its polished surface catching the light like a captured star. The cool weight of it feels substantial in his hand. He flips it over the inscription read, 'Family is who you make it' etched in elegant script, a whisper against the smooth metal.

He inhaled. "Wow, it's such a gracious gift, but I'm not your family."

"Wrong, son. I see how much they care for you as their own, and that's why you are *my* great-grandson."

Digi nods as Lyric helps him with the watch. He's so thin we're going to have to have it adjusted.

Grandpa's eyes crinkle at the corners as I lift the lid, the polished wood gleaming under the lamplight. Inside, nestled on faded velvet, lay sterling silver dog tags, cool and smooth to the touch. I trace the engraved inscription, the words a faint, raised relief. "Daddy... I may just be a tiny bump now, but I love you more than you ever know. Please keep this close to your heart until I can meet you and lay in your arms... Love, kisses and kicks from mommy's tummy." A faint scent of old leather and cedar hangs in the air as I close the box.

When I looked, Lyric was sobbing, and I felt choked up, too. I check the other dog tag and I see my last name and his with 'family' in script below it. A testament to both sides of my bloodline and to my future family.

"Wow, I don't know what to say. Thank you. It makes it seem more real that I have a family." I am holding back a dam of tears. It was almost as if I could hear my child's precious little voice whisper the words as I read them. Lyric gently fastened the clasp, the cool metal a contrast to my warm skin. I hold it proudly. "Thanks, grandpa."

"Wait, there's one more." He points to the box Lyric held.

"I had some help from your grandmother and the kid at the local pharmacy. I am not hip to technology," He looks at Digi's intricate computer setup, "but looks like my great-grandson could teach me a thing or two. What do you say?"

He chuckles. "No problem, grandpa."

Lyric lifted the lid, pushed aside the tissue paper, and gasped, holding up a sterling silver frame containing a photo of unfamiliar people. They must be....

"This is my side of your family and I wanted you, my grandchild, to have a reminder of who you came from. And the good thing about that photo is that it is the time my son did not take part. I so wanted to keep the negativity out of this visit, but..."

His face falls, and he sighs. "I'm going to the prison hospital to cut him off in person before I leave town. You want to accompany me? Maybe say a few last words? I understand if you don't, but maybe this will knock some sense into him."

In an instant, my anger returned, and I clenched my fists,

then ran my fingers through my hair before exhaling. It was whisper quiet, and I contemplated. Lyric rubbed my back while rubbing her stomach. I found that gesture comforting and if I needed to do this for anything; it was closure.

"Alright, let me get dressed. Digi order breakfast."

The scalding shower water, a stark contrast to the icy chill in my veins, soothed my tense muscles. I sighed, watching droplets cling to my beard. Then the shower door squeaked open, and she stepped in. My angel, her beauty igniting a fiery wave of desire. She stepped into the shower's arc, a delicious smile playing on her lips as the water cascaded over her. She looked so deliciously sexy and smiled as if she was reading my thoughts. My dirty, lust-filled thoughts.

"What about grandpa and Digi?"

She leans against me as the water splashes off her ass now, tugging my beard, pulling me down onto her waiting luscious lips. She tasted so sweet as I wrapped my arms around her.

She pulls back slightly. "Digi's teaching him how to download his photos from his phone to the cloud and they put on one of those obnoxiously loud violent movies sooo..." She trails off before palming me and I gasp. I watch her drop to her knees as she grips the base semi-tight. Her hand feels amazing, but her lips... are fucking magical.

"Oh baby, don't stop. Fuck!" I whisper yelled as she smirks then deep throats me with no hesitation. I almost came instantly. I had to switch it up. We were short on time, but I needed to feel her. I growl while I lift her to standing and then to my waist. She wraps her legs around me as I bounce her up and down, trying to hit the right combination.

She speeds up, trying to control this round, but I slap her

ass, causing her to stop. "Behave, kitten." I put her back on the ground.

She puts my hand on her breast. I immediately pinch and squeeze it and she moans.

"Please... more..." Her fingertips brush against my piercing. She looks at me wickedly, having done it on purpose. It was time to make my kitten purr.

I lift her, push her against the wall, and slide her down my shaft. She literally purrs to the feeling of me filling her up.

"Oh...so good, mmm. So fucking good." I feel like a dog in heat. Thrusting upward as I slammed her down. She bit her lip, trying to keep quiet. She would squeak occasionally, followed by panting. I keep her against the wall, speeding up as the heated water pours over us. I covered her mouth because she got louder. She covers mine, knowing that my grunts would give us away as well.

Her nails raked my back, thighs squeezed me harder, and her walls tightened around me. Her climax was coming. Knowing I had somewhere I had to be, though I didn't want to, the quicker I went, the sooner I could come back to my family. I sped up to coax her over the threshold. She bit my shoulder and moaned quietly as she came down from her high.

"Put me down."

My eyes follow as she kneels down to finish me off, as I was on the brink of climax. She licked and slurped around my throbbing member. I had to put my arm up against the wall as she sucked me to my breaking point.

"I'm so, so close, baby. Keep going...cum, cumming! I ugh ugh ugh!" She continued to suck me past orgasm and I almost crumpled to the floor. A smile played on her lips as her fingers curled around the soft sponge. The gentle squeak of it against my skin, then I returned the favor; the warm, soapy water gliding over every inch of her back. I lingered on her abdomen, feeling the smooth curve of her belly, the tiny bump beneath the sudsy lather.

She laughs at my concentration on her belly. "You're so adorable. Lord, help me if it's a girl because you're already protective."

"Damn right. My princess isn't dating until she's 40 or I'm dead." We step out and change for the day. I kept it simple, forgoing my cut, and wearing a black tank and blue jeans with boots.

"You're not wearing your club vest?" She raises her brow.

"Nah." I kiss her forehead. "No one needs to know about my brothers or me, and this is not a social visit. I need to get this off my chest to focus on the family I have, not the one that tried to kill me for money. I'll be back soon, okay?"

She holds my wrist that caresses her cheek and nods.

"I love you, kitten."

"I love you. Hurry home."

We walk out to grandpa and Digi, immersed in the movie.

"You ready?" My grandfather looks up and nods. He hugs Digi real tight.

"Until next time, kid. Let me know when you want to visit. I'm sure your parents won't mind. You'd love a place like L.A., the sights, the sounds, and pretty girls." He nudges him and you can see Digi openly blush at the 'girls' part.

"Okay, grandpa."

He hugs and kisses Lyric, placing his hand over her stomach, giving her words of encouragement. She basked in the fatherly advice and touch.

I kissed her one last time while talking to Digi.

"Take care of your mother while I'm gone." He agrees and we walk out to the elevator.

The drive to the Blackraven Humphrey correctional facility is 20 minutes south of town. While he drives, we talk about me mostly and my life here, the good, the bad, and the ugly. But it's the ugly that helped create me. I shared my vision with him: a beachfront wedding ceremony at our future home in San Diego, and of course, my grandmother and he would be there to witness it.

"Have you thought about what you're going to do about your mother's grave when you leave?"

I had thought about that for a while. "I'm going to move her to a beautiful plot overlooking the Pacific Ocean. She loved the water." I smile, reminiscing about us going to the water. She enjoyed watching me play while she listened to the calm ocean waves and enjoyed the salt-laden breeze.

He brings me out of my memories. "You miss her, don't you?"

"Absolutely. She was my first love and my only love for the longest, and now, I'm in love all over again. I know my mom had something to do with that. My heart is big like hers and I was protecting it from being hurt, from ending up like her."

He pats my leg. "You are certainly in love. It's all in how you look at her. It's pure, bask in it and hopefully, you'll have as many or more years than me and your grandmother. Also, if you would like we have a family plot in L.A. if you want to lay her there, up to you, just know it is an option."

I watched the landscape change from a vast barren desert to a cold metal compound in the middle of nowhere, surrounded by mountains and miles of barbed and electrified fencing.

Lyric

"We're going to need to cheer up your dad after he visits his father. I know, let's properly celebrate his birthday! I still feel awful. Let's go all out and make him feel loved!" It was the perfect surprise!

"Ummm...to be fair, they kidnapped and shot you, but I agree we should cheer him up. Let's go to the party store down the street and get some stuff to decorate the room with. Oh, and the Swiss bakery across the street to get red velvet and lemon cupcakes. Those are his favorites!"

With my purse in hand, we set off to create a memorable evening for my man.

Cupid

Why did I agree to do this shit again? Ugh. I've been fondled and searched to ensure I'm not here to finish what I started.

If they knew me, they would realize I only need my hands, but then I would be separated from my family, who are my life. He's barely worth this fucking visit, but I'm here for my grandfather.

The guards led us through three high security doors, each we had to get buzzed through. Here they held the general population; toward the rear, they housed the infirmary, each hospital space remaining a jail cell equipped to sustain any prisoner's condition.

The guards stop at a robin egg blue door with a small window and a trapdoor. They opened the door to which my dad's voice bellowed out immediately. "Why the fuck are you bothering me? I already ate! I don't want to be bothered by you degenerate assholes!"

My grandfather motions for me to stay back while he steps in. "Hello, son." If I assumed correctly, the color probably drained from his face. To face a parent after the despicable acts done and to get them to sympathize enough for them to rescue you is sad and pathetic.

"Dad, you made it. I-I thought you were supposed to be here two days ago? What the hell took you so long? Get me the hell out of here!"

He had some goddamn nerve talking to him like that! The urge to storm in, fists clenched, and silence his disrespect was overwhelming; a hot, angry flush burned my cheeks. But slow, deep breaths, the cool air filling my lungs, calmed the tempest. If Grandpa needed me, he would surely call.

"Oh, I was here, son. I spent that time fixing your goddamned mistakes! Doing what you should have been doing instead of disgracing this family. Come on in, Aleister."

I swear, the moment our eyes met, a chill colder than winter swept through the tiny cell, as if the very air itself had frozen.

"Why the fuck is he here? I'm in here because of you, you bastard!"

Wow, the audacity.

I lost it. "No, you're here because you were willing to kill your own son for money, you sick son of a bitch, so excuse the fuck out of me if I don't show any sympathy. I barely recognize you as a goddamn human being! You'll never be more than a useless sperm donor. Guess those days are over, aren't they?" I arch my brow, feeling victorious by that cheap shot.

His eyes blazed, wild and frantic. The sharp metallic *clink* of handcuffs against the cold steel bed frame echoed harshly in the cramped room, a jarring counterpoint to his strained, threatening posture.

"Scare tactics from half a man? Sorry, the only thing I

fear is becoming like you. I'll die before I let that happen. I have a woman who loves me and a child she is carrying, a child that I wanted, conceived out of love."

A flash of guilt hit him before he drew back into his icy demeanor, and I continued. "Yeah, you sick bastard, she was pregnant when you shot her and it's a miracle my girl and my baby are alive! How vile do you have to be to shoot a woman, let alone one carrying life? So, you see, I'll be fine without you. I already was. Grandpa, I'm going to wait in the sitting area. I have nothing more to say to this waste of life."

He holds my hand. "Wait, son. I want you to witness this. Carey, I've been more than patient, but what you did has shamed this family and I will not aid your behavior anymore. You are cut off from this family! You have no one to blame but yourself. I look forward to connecting with my grandson and his family. Everything you didn't do! I hope you learn how important family is over money. Goodbye."

"Dad, wait! Dad, no, you can't do this! You're going to choose that dirty bastard over your son?"

He turns back, and it is whisper quiet until, "I have no son." He walks out and I follow behind, never looking back. His pleading falls on deaf ears as we put more space between us.

My grandfather's last words to his son were powerful, a verbal severing of ties with his own flesh and blood. I know this hurts him so much. I give him a side hug as we walk out to the car. "It'll be okay, grandpa, maybe he'll understand after some time and make amends." He nods, obviously emotionally drained. I drove us back into town and insisted he have dinner with us before his flight in the morning. That brought the spark back.

We arrive at the hotel and take the private elevator up to my room.

"I wonder where they are. No one's been answering their phone. They must be shopping, probably baby clothes shopping. You know, she already has the baby's first week of..."

"SURPRISE! HAPPY BIRTHDAY!"

The light flickered on, revealing a dazzling array of gold and blue birthday decorations that shimmered and gleamed.

"What's all this? My birthday has passed."

We walk further in and she wraps her arms around me. "I knew you'd be upset after seeing your dad, and I wanted you to know how much your real family loves you. You mean the world to me, Digi, and especially our little one. I can't wait to make our family complete and official. I love you, Aleister."

She's all I needed; how could I not see it from day one? I think back to all that we shared and smiled.

"Thank you, kitten. I'm so lucky to have you and Digi in my life and our little nugget. And now I have my grandfather and a whole other side of the family to get to know. Most importantly, I'm spending it with the girl of my dreams. I can't wait... let's celebrate my life and our future..."

Six months later

"Honey, go sit on the patio and rest while we finish moving the rest of this furniture. That's all I need is for you to go into labor."

She waddles away. "Yeah, yeah, yeah, whatever. Just make sure the glider and ottoman face the bay window and the crib opposite the closet."

"Yes, dear." I smirk as she turns to glare at me before

enjoying the beachfront view of our new six-bedroom, four-bathroom villa.

The neighborhood was private and gated, with a wonderful semi-private beach. We gave Digi the second master bedroom opposite side of the house to our deluxe master bedroom.

His first major purchase was an all-black Camaro and then treated himself to a new wardrobe. He plans to upgrade his bike once he finds the perfect one. I was so proud; he was getting out and becoming more social. Soon enough, there would be a girl, maybe even two? Lyric told me not to rush, that even this progress was impressive.

Jackal and the rest of the boys stayed together and found a fraternity style house near the pier and amusement park. Their new home boasted eight bedrooms and four baths. A large, two-story garage housed their bikes, with the upper loft converted into a state-of-the-art gym. The finishing touch? A bar, reminiscent of the New Mexico clubhouse, with major upgrades.

They still had their hangout nights at the house, but spent a lot of time at popular local bars and chatting it up with other biker groups. They were fitting in so well, there was talk about getting new recruits.

Several hours later, after the guys left on their way to a rally, I was all alone with my girl. I find her still outside on the porch swing, listening to the ocean. The squeak of the door makes her turn her head towards me.

"Hey sweetheart, are you all done?" I pull her to my chest; the ocean breeze is a soothing caress as we rock together, the sound of the waves a gentle hush in the background. I couldn't help but kiss her temple and rub her belly.

"I just got her to calm down now. Don't rile up daddy's girl, please."

"Never, I want mommy as rested as she can be. You okay? Need anything, food, water, relaxing bubble bath?"

Her eyebrows raise. "Hmm, I think I will take you up on the bubble bath. Besides, you need to relax, too. You've been moving heavy stuff all day. Come on papa. Hey, where's Digi?"

"Oh, he's out with the guys. Will probably stay away tonight."

She eyes me. "Did you bribe him to stay away from his parent's house, to get me alone? Haven't you done enough?" She points to her full stomach. With a devilish grin, I kissed her hand. "I may have suggested he go out and have some fun, that's all. Hanging out alone with you is a bonus."

She tiptoed upstairs, entering our enormous walk-in closet to select sleepwear, pajamas for me, a sexy nightgown for her. Her pregnancy hasn't lessened her sex appeal. She still loves wearing seductive lingerie to bed. *That* is what will get her pregnant again.

I poured in some Epsom salts and dropped one of her bath bomb things. They are super girly, but they smell amazing. I selected a blue-green option; thankfully; it was glitter-free. The last one was pink, and I had glitter stuck in my beard for several days. That went well at the clubhouse.

I started the jets to get the water going when she walked in, putting our clothes on the counter. "Unzip me, please." She faced away as I gently pulled the zipper for her sunflower dress down and let it crumple at her feet before she stepped out. From her seat on the edge, she swung her legs over and slid into the water with a blissful sigh.

I groan, trying not to take her. I had to be honest. In the

beginning, I was afraid I'd hurt the baby even though time and time again she reassured me that the baby would be fine. That it could help aid in the delivery process.

Still, I find it creepy, not that I haven't taken her, because I have, repeatedly. With the plan of christening every square inch of this house minus my son's space. I guess it's first-time dad worries.

I remove all my clothing as she rests against the tub, eyeing me and licking her lips. I pull my hair up into a man bun.

"You look so damn sexy, baby." She winks as she sits back against the opposite side of the tub, letting me sink in. She rubs my tired sore muscles, and it feels amazing.

"Are you as shocked as me at what it took for us to get here? To think I almost punched Johnny in the face at the bar. Had I reacted like I wanted, maybe everything would have been different, but I like the path chosen. I have my son, my baby girl will be here soon, and I have my overly loving boyfriend."

Reaching over into my jeans pocket, I grinned. "I'd change one thing, though. Your last name."

I opened the box to reveal a breathtaking princess-cut diamond and emerald ring, its facets sparkling brilliantly in the light.

"Lyric Celeste Pullman, will you become the future Mrs. McElroy? I swear I'll love you forever and beyond. You've changed this stubborn, love hating biker into a caring man filled with love and anticipation as we wait for little Xaria Lennox to make her debut. What do you say, kitten?"

I watched her lip tremble, a single tear escaping and tracing a path down her cheek as she fought to hold back her excitement. "Oh baby, it's what I've been waiting for! Yes!

Yes, I'll marry you!" She jumps up, splashing water everywhere to wrap her arms around me and kiss me urgently. I
kiss and caress her. I'd worry about the cleanup later. Right
now, I was basking because this woman was now my fiancée,
one step closer to being my wife.

She squeals in laughter. "Oh baby, I'm so happy! I love
you, Aleister. You're my very own Cupid."

That I am, kitten, that I am.

Lyric

One year later

What a year! Well, more than a year, really.

Our journey started 14 months ago, after an extraordinary and unexpected series of events. I mean, come on!

I went from being abandoned to waitress to bar owner.

My honey bunny and I butted heads bad about the bar, but I guess it was a saving grace that it burned down.

I'd never tell him that, though. I'd never hear the end of it.

Then I was a hostage, a gunshot victim, girlfriend, fiancée, and now mother.

Little Miss Xaria Lennox aka nugget made her big debut about a week after we settled into our home. Sneaky girl, too. My water broke while I was asleep. I was so exhausted carrying my baby girl around, I barely noticed. If Aleister hadn't been snuggled up next to me, I probably would have delivered the baby at home.

I'm always amazed to see grown men, tough guys even, cry at the sight of a baby. There were actual tears, but it was wonderful to have her uncles there for her arrival.

And now...

"Cupid... Cupid! I'm never going to be ready in time!" I turned the corner to see Jackal and Ms. Alana all snuggled up. Ms. Alana is Jackal's new ol' lady and possibly the sweetest woman ever. She is like a mother to me and loves my kids to death.

Their love story is adorable. They met at the newly opened coffee shop!

I know, right? So cute!

And it was downhill from there. I know he still holds a flame for Ms. Paige, but I believe it was she who sent Ms. Alana to confront him. He is completely smitten and seeing him smile with her melts my heart.

"Ms. Alana, can you watch Xar? I'm nowhere near ready and I can't find her daddy."

"Of course dear, you know you never have to ask me to watch my grandbaby. Come here, sugar, come to your grandma! Now go, you're going to give him heart palpitations if you're late!"

She shoos me off and I make my way to the parlor.

Cupid

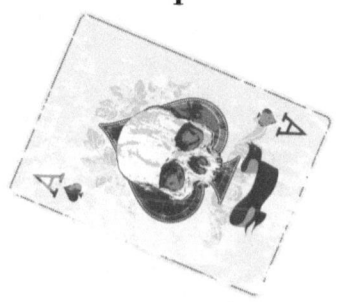

I can't even fathom what has happened in the past year of my life. I swore I'd never fall in love on a stack of bibles soaked in holy water, but now... well, I'm glad I was just a stubborn fool and she didn't take any lip from me. She dug her heels in and won my heart. I am proud to be a father to Digi and Xaria.

We made the adoption legal for Digi about six months after the move when we got a solid schedule down for Xar. My life is complete with my son, daughter, and amazing wife to be.

I watch the waves crash against the shore. I love the sound of the water. It reminds me that my mom is around, watching over me. Lyric and I sometimes sit, close our eyes, and listen. She'd squeeze my hand, and that was her silent way of saying how much she loved me.

"Cupid! Hey, man..." I come back to the present as Cheetah snaps his fingers to get me to focus.

"Huh? What?"

"Where the hell did you go? Get it together We're on a schedule. Let me look at you."

I stand up, but I'm still fidgeting.

"Perfect, man. Come on, let's take our places. It's time to get you married."

Lyric

"Lia, you are a godsend! Wow."

I gaze in the mirror as she sets down her brush. Stunning! No clown makeup here. She perfectly captured the simple beach vibe I wanted. My hair is loosely curled, windswept and dreamy; it's even better than I imagined. I fanned myself.

"Lyric, don't you dare start crying! All my hard work will not be ruined until the end."

Breathe Lyric... just breathe.

After a few minutes, I calmed down. "Lia, Jess, can you help me with the dress, please?"

"Of course. What are your girls for?"

Cupid

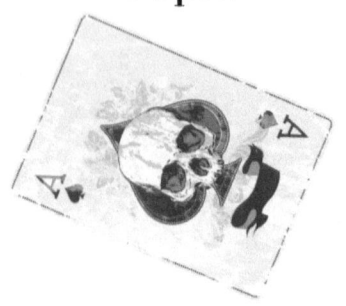

The world is moving unbelievably slow, feels like someone hit the super slo-mo button. The only saving grace is the gentle salt-infused breeze hitting my face.

Cheetah nudges me. "You okay? Don't get me killed because you decided to pass out."

I shake my head and bend my knees a bit. "No way... wouldn't miss this moment for anything in the world."

Lyric

Everything is done. The photographer just finished the first look session and heads outside to set up for the ceremony.

Knock knock

"Mom, it's me."

I turn to see my handsome son opening the door, looking so handsome in his suit. He instantly wipes his tears, and I feel mine coming.

"Don't make me cry!" I scream.

"I'm sorry, you look so beautiful. Come on, you've got a date with destiny."

I was a bit confused. "I thought Jackal was going to escort me?"

He shakes his head. He had grown into himself, more confident and gaining muscle every day. He's getting to be quite the flirt, but I keep him grounded on how to respect a girl. He assures me he knows. He better! He's a reflection of me.

"No, I insisted on taking the honor of giving my mother away. You've done so much and given me everything I wanted. It's my honor to be the one who ushers you from girl-friend to wife." I only nod because a flood of tears will follow any words.

He holds his arm out and I wrap my arm around his and hold my bouquet of white lilies in my other hand as we walk down the stairs of our house to the beach out back.

Cupid

WOW!

Bright sunlight glinted off her hair, a halo framing a face that I would allow to take my last breath. My heart hammered a frantic rhythm against my ribs. She was breath taking, radiant, stunning and utterly, completely mine.

She was a vision in white chiffon lace. The delicate fabric whispered against her skin as she moved, the split front revealing glimpses of tanned legs. The off-the-shoulder style showcased the elegant curve of her neck, and the long train pooled around her like a silken cloud. It was breathtaking. She went barefoot, and I did too, with my khaki pants cuffed and white button-down.

Digi smiled proudly, walking his mother down the aisle. He had grown into his own, found a bachelor pad because he didn't want to cramp our style, especially with Xaria being there, but we kept his room the way he left it and invited him over for dinner as much as we could without interfering in his social life.

My boy is a heartbreaker, I can feel it. Of course, he

won't tell us. We're his parents, but I've seen a couple of different girls in his company. Maybe his club name should be Cupid. Pass down the legacy.

Before I realize it, they're in front of me and he whispers something in her ear. She nods before he kisses her hand, then her cheek. I hold out my hand and he places her hand in mine.

Our eyes meet and I'm done. I can't hold back my happy tears. She wipes them with a handkerchief she had cleverly hidden in her bouquet, blotting her own eyes to not ruin her makeup.

I could have told her just how gorgeous she was, her eyes sparkling like the ocean, her smile as bright as the sun, but all I got out was, "Hi."

She giggled and her smile was worth my brain lapse. I could hear chuckles behind me from my groomsmen, Cheetah and Knox.

We kept the bridal party small with two each. Lia and Jess were recent additions to the family. They all met at a weekend rally downtown and became fast friends. They were her support system after Xar was born. She went to them for advice, since Lia had two boys and Jess, a little girl.

She was comfortable around us guys, but she craved female friendships for deeper connection, and I'm so happy she found them.

Lyric

He's so adorable, the man I now call my husband. The ceremony went off without a hitch. Even the wind died down a bit. I'm happy to walk back down the aisle with my love, my husband.

The reception was under a breathtaking ivory tent shimmering under the warm setting sun, close to the house. We sat at the head table, the murmur of conversation a gentle hum after navigating the lively reception line. I feed my handsome husband as he plays with his daughter. She giggles and coos to his every movement. I grab his attention. "Hey, one more bite. I have to feed her, too."

He leans forward for a bite and a sweet kiss. Then he's staring at me.

"What? Is it my makeup?"

I almost panic thinking I ruined the amazing job Lia did, but he shakes his head.

Cupid

"No, I just want to look into the gorgeous eyes of my stunning wife. You're absolutely the most beautiful girl on this Earth, and I love you."

That did it, and she cried while smiling. Xaria takes my finger and I wiggle it, causing her to coo. She looks at me in her cute pink ruffle dress and matching socks.

"Daaa... da da!" ***Squeal***

We stared in astonishment. "Did she just..."

"Oh, my god! She said dada, she said her first word! Xar, say dada again!" Lyric coaxes her.

"Da, da, da, da!" She screams the last one enough to catch everyone's attention.

"I'm her first word! She said dada!" I pull Lyric in for a kiss and then I kiss Xar on the forehead. This was the icing on the cake. After everyone applauded, Lyric took the mic.

Lyric

"Thank you, everyone, for being here on our special day, and apparently, to witness Xar's first word. Now we know she's truly a daddy's girl. That's a good thing to know. I suppose in seven months or so we'll find out if we have another daddy's girl or perhaps we will finally get a junior..." I pause for reaction.

Everyone gasped, and he dropped his glass, visibly shocked. The sharp breaking noise spooked Xar a little.

My emotions were overwhelming as I sniffled to avoid the tears. "Surprise! We're having another baby."

Alana takes Xaria as he cups my face. "Really, kitten? Another baby?" I place his hand on my barely there bump.

"Pretty sure, same symptoms as last time and four confirmed pregnancy tests. You said she wouldn't be the only one. What do you think now?"

Cupid

I slam my lips onto hers. What a way to end a perfect day!

I realize she's being pulled away by her bridesmaids and they all hug and cry. Watching them beam over the news and patting her stomach, I wonder why I hadn't picked up on it.

I suspect it happened the night Digi moved out, and she wanted to run through the house naked. Albeit an odd request, I indulged her in it. Then I indulged in her, in every room.

Afterwards, Xaria started to stir on the baby monitor, and Lyric made her way to our daughter's room. "Mommy duties call. I'll see you in bed?"

I watch her saunter out and eventually follow her to see her breastfeeding our precious angel. I sat on the floor next to the rocker she was in. She wiggles her tiny hand while she suckles on her nipple. It's the most beautiful thing ever. She catches me licking my lips.

"You're incorrigible. If you hadn't realized it, you probably knocked me up again."

I smile, "Would be okay with me." She rolls her eyes and laughs.

And I did. Now I'm gazing at my new wife and my newest bundle growing within her while I look at my handsome son and hold my beautiful girl whose first word was "dada".

Love is truly all I needed.

About the Author

Thank you for taking the time to read The Black Aces. I hope you enjoyed the book and would love if you could leave a review

on any retailer or Goodreads.

If you would like to hear more from me about new releases and sales, you can visit my website.

Website: https://www.scourtneybooks.com/

Or follow my FB group: S Courtney'sBook Nook

www.ingramcontent.com/pod-product-compliance
Lightning Source LLC
Chambersburg PA
CBHW022029240626
47154CB00007B/2323